THE LOWER DEPTHS

THE LOWER DEPTHS

MAXIM GORKY

Translated by
Kitty Hunter-Blair and Jeremy Brooks

With an Introduction by Edward Braun
and a Preface by Jeremy Brooks

A Richard Seaver Book

THE VIKING PRESS · NEW YORK

Maxim Gorky

1868 Born, Alexey Maximovich Peshkov, in Nizhni Novgorod, 225 miles east of Moscow. Mother from a family of dyers, father an upholsterer, later a wharf manager.

1872 Father dies. Mother abandons Alexey, who is brought up by Grandmother.

1878 Mother dies. Grandfather sends the boy away to earn his own living.

1878–1884 Nomadic labourer – boot boy, errand boy, bird catcher, dishwasher on a Volga paddleboat, assistant in an icon shop. Self-education begins.

1884 Arrives in Kazan, hoping to enter University, but fails to get a place. Works as stevedore, meets students, intellectuals, revolutionaries. Works in a bakery. Toys with Populism, Tolstoyism, dreams of setting up a Tolstoyan commune. Is invited to become a police spy. Studies the violin, tries to fall in love, fails at both. News of Grandmother's death reaches him.

1887 Tries to commit suicide, succeeds in damaging left lung.

1888 Working in an up-Volga fishery, then as railway nightwatchman. Arrives in Moscow, horrified by it, heads back towards Nizhni Novgorod. Calls at Yasnaya Polyana, is given rolls and coffee in the kitchen by Tolstoy's wife. Is beaten nearly to death by Cossacks for trying to intercede for an adulteress who is being dragged naked behind a horse. Is hospitalized.

1889 Attempts to enrol as an army engineer, rejected as politically unreliable. Shows his writings to elderly Populist writer Korolenko, whose gentle criticisms cause him to tear up his MSS and resolve never to write again. Succeeds in falling in love with a married woman, Olga.

1892 Runs away from Olga to Tiflis, and a job on a local newspaper, which publishes his first story, *Makar Chudra*.

is allowed to be performed for subscribers of the Art Theatre only, with uniformed police as ticket collectors. In the provinces the play provokes riots. Gorky's nickname changed to 'Stormy Petrel'.

Dec. 1902   *The Lower Depths* staged in Moscow – 'thrilled and stirred' the middle-class audience, then sweeps the world's capitals. 75,000 copies of the play sold in a year. Gorky's American publisher states that his fame now surpasses Tolstoy's. Gorky turns over much of his private funds to the Social Democratic Party, after meeting some of Lenin's followers in Moscow.

1903   'Knowledge' becomes a co-operative publishing house.

1904   Writes *Summer Folk*, a play heavily influenced by Chekhov.

1905   Is involved with the priest, Gapon, in organizing the workers' march on the Winter Palace. Joins delegation of intellectuals to the Minister of the Interior to plead for no violence. After the slaughter of 'Bloody Sunday' Gapon flees to Gorky's apartment, is disguised, leaves Russia. Two days later Gorky is arrested, imprisoned in the Peter and Paul Fortress, where he writes *Children of the Sun*, one of his best plays. Pressure from the West, and bail money from a power-mad industrialist who thought he could 'buy the revolution', gets him out of prison.

Dec. 1905   Involved in organizing support for the workers' barricades in Moscow during the last gasp of the '1905 Revolution'. Pursued by police, he flees to Finland, thence to Berlin.

1906   What was to have been a triumphal fund-raising tour of the United States aborted by press disclosures that the 'Mme Gorky' he lives with is not his wife, but a Moscow Art Theatre actress. Publicly spurned by the famous, Gorky goes into retreat, writes *The Mother*, a novel welcomed by Lenin as 'an instrument of revolution'. Completes *Enemies*. Settles on Capri.

1907   *Enemies* staged by Max Reinhardt at the Kleines Theater, Berlin. Attends Fifth Congress of Social

Democratic Party in Brussels and London. Is not (and never became) a member of the Party. Meets Lenin and Trotsky. Returns to Capri, writes two novels.

1908   Writes *The Confession*, reveals his religious attitude towards revolution. With Bogdanov and Lunacharsky sets up a school for revolutionary Russian workers. Leading Mensheviks, suspecting Gorky's attachment to Lenin, refuse to come and lecture; Lenin, angry about *The Confession*, and preparing to expel Bogdanov from the Party, also refuses to come.

1909   Constant correspondence from Lenin, who fosters factionalism at the school, succeeds in driving Bogdanov out.

1910   Lenin visits Capri. Gorky writes two more novels.

1911–1912   Remains in retreat on Capri, writing many stories, including the powerful *Twenty-six and One*. His play, *Vassa Zheleznova* (*The Mother*) awarded Griboyedov Prize in Moscow.

1913   Writes *Childhood*, published serially in a newspaper. On the 300th anniversary of the Romanov dynasty an amnesty for political exiles is granted. Gorky returns cautiously to Russia. Breaks with Lenin, who keeps writing friendly letters but gets no replies

1914–1917   Writes several autobiographical works. Opposes Russia's participation in the Great War. Founds two magazines and a newspaper, *New Life*, which becomes the most widely read newssheet among the intelligentsia. Attacked as a Bolshevik and pro-German by the Right, and as a proponent of 'false unification' by the Leninist Left. After the February 1917 Revolution, opposes Lenin's plans for a further Bolshevik uprising.

1918–1921   *New Life* the only independent journal in Russia. Gorky continues to oppose the new regime, attacks Lenin as 'the mad chemist'. *New Life* finally forced to close down. Gorky allows himself to be reconciled with Lenin. But Zinoviev, an old enemy, is after Gorky's blood; Lenin pleads with him to leave Russia 'to recuperate'.

1922–1924   Travels about Europe. Writes a film scenario, *Stepan Razin*, which is a clear condemnation of Lenin's attitudes, and his *Reminiscences* of Tolstoy, Chekhov and Andreyev.

1924–1930   Settles in Sorrento. Visited by his legal wife and their son. Writes *My Universities, Fragments*. Is mercilessly sponged on by other exiles.

1928   Nizhni Novgorod renamed Gorky – part of Stalin's campaign to persuade Gorky to return to Russia. Gorky visits Russia and is given red carpet treatment.

1929   Another visit to Russia. Gorky shown a huge collective farm and a 'humane' concentration camp – both specially prepared for his benefit.

1931–1932   Completes three last plays, *Somov and Others, Yegor Bulchychov and Others* and *Dostigayev and Others*. Returns to Russia for good. Is given funds to start publishing houses, magazines, writers' collectives.

1933   Gorky now a 'superintendent of writers'.

1934   Head of Writers' Union. His son, Maxim, dies – almost certainly liquidated.

1935   Rewrites his early plays, *The Zikovs* and *The Last Ones*, so that both plays reflect his knowledge that the Revolution had somehow gone wrong. He applies for a passport, is refused.

1936   Second application for a passport refused. Gorky knows that time has run out for him. Stalin is preparing the ground for the Great Purges, can't afford to have someone of Gorky's international weight around. On 19th June Gorky dies, in circumstances never clarified. By the end of the year, all who attended his death are also dead.

Introduction

Gorky was thirty-two when he was introduced by Chekhov to the Moscow Art Theatre company at Yalta in the spring of 1900. His first collection of stories had recently been published, selling over 100,000 copies and winning for him a popularity enjoyed only by Tolstoy and Chekhov himself amongst living writers in Russia. Already Gorky was kept under constant surveillance by a regime disturbed at his unique influence over the young and at the fervour with which he championed the poor and the underprivileged. As yet he had no declared party allegiance, but he had spent the first of several spells in prison for 'spreading sedition'.

Russia at the turn of the century was seething with social unrest and the government, rightly fearful of the threat posed by the left-wing intelligentsia, was quick to seize on any pretext for the ruthless suppression of dissent. So far the theatre, controlled on the one hand by a vigilant censor and on the other by commercial interests and middle-class dilettantism, had scarcely responded to the mood of the times; but now Chekhov realized that Gorky might become the dramatist that Russia lacked. The Art Theatre's directors, Stanislavsky and Nemirovich-Danchenko, were easily persuaded and with their encouragement Gorky was soon considering the idea of scenes depicting 'a lodging house, foul air, trestle-beds, a long dreary winter' and called initially 'Without Sunlight'. But before long he had begun work on a second play, *Philistines*, which was completed first in September 1901. Gorky was persuaded that it would be wiser to submit *Philistines* to the censor rather than wait until he had completed *The Lower Depths*, a work whose compassionate portrayal of rogues and vagabonds was precisely the kind of subject that had already gained him such notoriety. So it was that *Philistines*, a play with far more overt political implications, was staged first in March 1902. It depicts the pettiness of the Russian lower-middle class in contrast with the vigour and optimism of the 'new man' of proletarian stock. With apprehension verging on paranoia, the authorities policed the select first-night subscription audience with agents clumsily disguised as ushers in evening dress. Almost inevitably the production itself proved a decorous anti-climax, partly because of the mutilation wrought on the text by the censor, partly because of the play's own looseness of form, but not least because of the company's failure to grasp its social significance. On Chekhov at least its meaning was not lost; referring to the play in 1903 he wrote:

> Gorky is the first in Russia and in the world at large to have expressed contempt and loathing for the petty bourgeoisie and he has done it at the precise moment when Russia is ready for protest.*

Despite a further spell in jail and temporary exile in remote Arzamas, Gorky completed *The Lower Depths* in the summer of 1902, some eight months after *Philistines*. Again the censor demanded major surgery:

> It is absolutely essential to change the policeman Medvediev into an ordinary retired soldier, since the participation of a custodian of the law in the escapades of the inmates of a doss house is inadmissable on the stage. The end of Act Two must be substantially shortened to remove out of respect for the deceased woman the indelicate conversation which follows her death. Cuts are required in the speeches of the pilgrim – in particular his remarks concerning God, the after-life, deception and so on. Finally, the various crude or indecent expressions throughout the play must be removed.†

In Nemirovich-Danchenko's opinion the play was only passed finally (with some eighty cuts) because the authorities were convinced that it would fail anyway. If so, it was a monumental miscalculation: the opening night in Moscow on 18th December 1902, with Stanislavsky himself playing Satin and Chekhov's wife Olga Knipper as Nastya, equalled the triumph of *The Seagull* in the same theatre four years earlier. The house was in an uproar at the final curtain and a bewildered Gorky took over fifteen calls. Although differing widely in their interpretations, the Moscow critics were unanimous in their praise of both play and production. Chekhov's response was more qualified; in July 1902 he wrote to Gorky:

* Letter to Sumbatov-Yuzhin, 26 February 1903.
† *Polnoe sobranie sochinenii* (Moscow, 1970), vol. VII, p. 606.

It is new and without question good. Act Two is especially fine – the best, the strongest, and when I read it, above all the end, I almost jumped with pleasure. ... You have left the most interesting characters out of Act Four (apart from the Actor) and you would do well to consider what you lose by that.

Then he added admiringly 'the Actor's death is terrifying. You hit the spectator in the face without warning.' But to others he gave the opinion that it would have been better treated as a short story and that he didn't like Gorky behaving 'like a priest'.

Initially Gorky was delighted with the production which captured totally the atmosphere of the Moscow slums and faithfully re-created the characters of the down-and-outs who had been Gorky's close comrades in his youth. But soon he had second thoughts about both the play and its reception; in particular he was concerned at the significance of the pilgrim Luka who was generally taken to be the embodiment of brotherly love, with little account given to his hurried departure at the first sign of real trouble or to the trail of ruin and disillusion that he leaves in his wake. In 1903 Gorky said in an interview:

In the play there is no opposition to what Luka says. The basic question that I wanted to pose was: what is better, truth or compassion? What is more necessary? Should compassion be carried to the point where it involves deception, as in Luka's case? This is not a subjective matter but a question of universal philosophy. Luka represents compassion to the point of deception as a means of salvation, but there is in the play no representative of truth to oppose him. Kleshch, the Baron, Pepel are facts of life – and one needs to distinguish between facts and the truth, which are far from one and the same thing. ...*

Significantly Gorky makes no mention here of Satin. Some time before, he had written 'Satin's speech about truth is pallid. But apart from Satin there is nobody to give it to, and he is incapable of expressing it more clearly. As it stands, it sounds strange coming from him.'†

* Interview in *Peterburgskaya gazeta*, 15. vi. 1903.
† Letter to Piatnitsky, August 1902.

Although hastily banned from performance in all other Russian theatres *The Lower Depths* continued to run with huge success at the Moscow Art Theatre, and in fact the production there remains scarcely altered to this day. In 1903 it was staged at Reinhardt's Kleines Theater in Berlin with Reinhardt himself as Luka, and played for over five-hundred performances. In the same year it was given its London premiere by the Stage Society, then two years later Lugné-Poe directed it in Paris with Eleonora Duse as Vassilissa. Since then it has been constantly in the international repertoire and has been twice filmed: by Jean Renoir in 1936 as *Les Bas-fonds* with Louis Jouvet as the Baron and Jean Gabin as Pepel, and by Kurosawa in 1957 with Toshiro Mifune as Pepel.

Gorky was always prepared to rework his plays to modify or clarify their meaning (notably *Enemies* to which he gave a significantly different political slant for its Soviet revival in 1933), but he never returned to *The Lower Depths* and it remains as it was originally written – ambiguous and inconclusive. When he wrote it in 1902 he had no choice: the conflict between truth and compassion, between harsh facts and the beautiful lie was within himself. Soon he sought to resolve it by embracing the activist cause of Marxism and by pursuing the truth in a series of socially committed works of which *Enemies* is perhaps the least compromising. Yet his characters remained, like Kleshch, the Baron and Pepel, 'facts of life', complex human beings who transcend dogmatic schematization. In *Enemies* even the unscrupulous factory boss, Mikhail Skrobotov, is treated with a compassion that Gorky manages still to reconcile with the inescapable social truth of the play.

If *The Lower Depths* is Gorky's most humane, hence most inconclusive play, it is by no means a play apart: like all his work it proceeds from the man himself, reflecting his own complexity and his own honest doubt. About one thing only Gorky was never in doubt: as Satin says 'Man! There's the truth for you! What is man? It isn't me – or you – or them . . . no! It's you and me and them and the old man and Mahomet . . . all rolled into one.' To that extent he was a political writer.

EDWARD BRAUN

This introduction appeared originally in *Flourish*, 1972, issue 1.

Preface: The 1972 Translation

The same team of directors, designers and translators approached the RSC's 1972 production of *The Lower Depths* as had the previous year collaborated successfully on Gorky's lesser-known play, *Enemies*. But the problems we now faced were entirely different. For where *Enemies* is a piece of social realism – 'the missing link', as Ronald Bryden described it, 'between Chekhov and the Russian Revolution' – calling for a style of translation and performance rooted in a recognizable social milieu, *The Lower Depths* is a dark and brooding poem illuminated from within by lightning flashes of wit and dazzling bursts of boisterousness. Verbally it is so packed and rich that language has to be stretched to accommodate it; and visually one has to find concrete equivalents for the recurring images that weave sinuously through the text.

The images – of light and dark, constraint and freedom, truth and lies, reality and dreams – are not what the play is 'about', any more than the generally accepted encapsulation – 'the human condition at the bottom of society' – is what it's 'about'. Poems are not 'about' anything – or, rather, they are about something different for everyone who encounters them. It's true that Gorky's title, of which the most accurate translation would be 'At the Bottom', does give some sort of licence to view the play as social comment. But the nearest thing to a recognizable 'message' in the play is Satin's famous speech about 'Man' in Act Four, and the fact that it is delivered by a half-drunk, penniless card-sharper in a cold, dark and empty cellar can hardly be taken to mean that Gorky considered such a life-style an essential condition for understanding humanity in this way, since the same view is propounded over and over again, through many mouthpieces, throughout Gorky's writing. It is an expression of one of his deepest beliefs, but it is no more his 'message' in this play than is Luka's determination to tell every one of the hopeless down-and-outs in the cellar the thing that will most comfort them, regardless of truth and regardless of result. Luka's enigmatic character, and the powerful effect, for both good and ill, that he has on the other characters, is an important element in the play, but it is only one of many strands that are being woven together to form a pattern that has its own unique meaning: a meaning which is not to be analysed, since it can only be expressed by the play itself.

Many of these strands are made up not of 'significant action' but of verbal repetitions, of word-play, and of the counterpointing of half-expressed ideas which eventually, as in any poem, coalesce to illuminate an idea never itself directly expressed. This verbal complexity throws a heavy responsibility on the translator. Accuracy, and an ear for natural dialogue, are not enough. An attempt has to be made, fraught with danger though it is, to find ways of matching Gorky's exuberant inventiveness and his loving play with the textures and resonances of words. Often one has to admit failure. The character of a language grows out of, and alongside of, the character of a nation, and equips itself to express nuances of thinking and feeling that may be exclusive to that nation – part of the nation's 'soul'. No inventiveness on a translator's part can overcome the fact that in Russian the word 'chelovek' means 'man' both in the individual sense of 'one human soul', 'a person', 'a man', 'a woman', and in the sense of 'humankind', and, since Russian has no definite nor indefinite articles, it can be used in both senses at once, to produce a resonance unobtainable in English.

This is no excuse for not trying to make up, in some other way, for what is inevitably lost; and we have tried, sometimes perhaps with results with which a Russian expert would not agree. But there's no help for it: Gorky's best interests would not be served by a cautious, dry accuracy, which would enfeeble the closely woven riches of the text. If we have sometimes gone beyond what a rigorous exegesis of the original can justify, it is only in the hope of thereby making up for what is lost elsewhere.

There is one area, however, in which we have thought it best to play safe. Some of the characters have names which are obvious nicknames connected with their appearance, character or occupation. With others the names merely suggest, through affinity, that character's essential nature. Attempts to duplicate this in English have failed. With a few of the names a solution can be found – Kvashnia, for instance, could be called 'Dumpling', Krivoy Zob could be 'Flopchin' – but it's a dangerous game: 'Dumpling' isn't *quite* right, it suggests too soft and dimple-cheeked a character, and 'Pastry' has overtones of 'Pasty', which is again wrong. And if one isn't careful an altogether too whimsical aura starts to infiltrate the play. However, for any director who likes to create problems for himself, Kitty Hunter-Blair has provided the following ingredients:

Kostyliov — 'kostyl' means 'crutch' – he is an old man, stiff in the joints.

Medvediev — 'Medved' is a bear, very appropriate for this bumbling policeman.

Pepel — the thief whose life has gone sour on him: the word means 'ashes'.

Kvashnia — the hawker of dumplings ('pelmeni' – a sort of ravioli). The name means dough, or the wooden trough in which dough is kneaded; can also be used of a slow, flabby person, which Kvashnia is not.

Luka — some echo of 'lukaviy' – cunning. Also possibly in Gorky's mind was Luka, the doctor/evangelist.

Krivoy Zob — literally, 'crooked jowl' – he presumably has a goiter, and in some translations has been called thus. He and his friend the Tartar are probably long-shoremen at an inland port – Gorky himself was once so employed. The word for porter derives from the hooks with which they carried their loads.

In the RSC production certain cuts were made in the text, sometimes to help with the pacing of a scene but more commonly, and regretfully, for reasons of length of playing time. These have been indicated by square brackets [thus]. The one or two minor additions which were made in the staging are indicated by round brackets (thus).

I would like to acknowledge the contribution made by David Jones, the director, in preparing this text for production.

JEREMY BROOKS

This translation of The Lower Depths *was first performed by the Royal Shakespeare Company on 29th June 1972, at the Aldwych Theatre, with the following cast:*

MIKHAIL IVANOV KOSTYLIOV, *aged 54,* *landlord of a doss-house*	Tony Church
VASSILISSA KARPOVNA, *his wife, aged 26*	Heather Canning
NATASHA, *her sister, aged 20*	Lisa Harrow
ABRAM IVANICH MEDVEDIEV, *their uncle,* *a policeman, aged 50*	Richard Mays
VASSILY PEPEL, *aged 28*	Mike Pratt
ANDREY MITRICH KLESHCH, *a locksmith,* *aged 40*	Morgan Shepherd
ANNA, *his wife, aged 24*	Lynn Dearth
NASTYA, *a streetwalker*	Alison Fiske
KVASHNIA, *a dumpling peddler, aged 40*	Lila Kaye
BUBNOV, *a cap-maker, aged 45*	Peter Geddis
BARON, *aged 33*	Richard Pasco
SATIN, *aged close to 40*	Bernard Lloyd
ACTOR, *aged close to 40*	Peter Woodthorpe
LUKA, *aged 60, a palmer*	Gordon Gostelow
ALYOSHKA, *aged 20, a cobbler*	Nicholas Grace
TARTAR ⎱ *'hook-men', or porters*	Robert Ashby
KRIVOY ZOB ⎰	David Calder
Various paupers, without names or speech	Ted Valentine
	Marion Lines

Directed by David Jones
Designed by Timothy O'Brien
Costumes by Tazeena Firth and Timothy O'Brien

THE LOWER DEPTHS

Act One

A cellar, which looks like a cave. The ceiling consists of heavy stone arches, black with smoke and with the plaster falling. The light comes in from the audience, and downwards from a square window on the right. The right-hand corner is taken up by PEPEL's *room, separated from the rest by a thin partition, close to the door of which is* BUBNOV's *plank bed. In the left-hand corner is a large Russian stove; in the stone wall, left, a door leads to the kitchen in which* KVASHNIA, *the* BARON *and* NASTYA *live. Against the wall, between the stove and the door, stands a wide bed covered with a dirty chintz canopy. Plank beds stand all the way around the walls.*

In the foreground by the left wall stands a block of wood with a vice and a small anvil fixed to it; in front of it is another, slightly smaller, block, on which KLESHCH *is sitting, trying keys in old locks. At his feet lie two large bunches of keys of different sizes, held together by rings made of bent wire; a battered tin samovar; a hammer; files. In the middle of the lodging house stand a large table, two benches, and a stool, all unpainted and dirty. At the table* KVASHNIA *is in charge of the samovar, the* BARON *is chewing black bread, and* NASTYA, *on the stool, is reading a tattered book, her elbows on the table. On the bed covered by the canopy* ANNA *is lying, and can be heard coughing.* BUBNOV *sits on his bed, holding a hat-block between his knees, and trying to work out how best to cut the old, unpicked pair of trousers which he has pulled over the block. Beside him lie a cardboard hatbox – torn to make cap peaks – some pieces of oil-cloth, rags.* SATIN *has just woken up. He lies on his plank bed, growling. On the stove, out of sight the* ACTOR *is tossing and coughing.*

Early Spring. Morning.

BARON. Further – further!
KVASHNIA. Well, so I said, 'Oh no, my dear,' I said, 'you get

away from me with all that kind of talk,' I said, 'I've been through all that once, and I'm not going through it again. You won't catch me taking that bridal veil again, not for a hundred baked crabs I won't!'

BUBNOV (*to* SATIN). What are you snorting about?

SATIN snorts some more.

KVASHNIA. 'I'm a free woman,' I said, 'I earn my own living,' I said, 'why should I go and get myself written into another body's passport? Lock myself up in some man's rotten dungeon?' I said. 'Oh, no!' No, I tell you, I wouldn't marry him, not if he was an American prince.

KLESHCH. You're lying.

KVASHNIA. Wha-a-at?

KLESHCH. You're a liar. You'll marry Abramka.

The BARON *grabs* NASTYA's *book and reads the title.*

BARON. 'Fatal Love'.

He roars with laughter. NASTYA *reaches for the book.*

NASTYA. Give it here, give it back! Come on, stop bloody fooling!

The BARON *watches her, waving the book about beyond her reach.*

KVASHNIA (*to* KLESHCH). You red-headed goat, I'll give you 'liar'! You've got a nerve, talking to me like that!

BARON (*bringing the book down on* NASTYA's *head*). You're an idiot, Nastya.

NASTYA. Give it here. (*She grabs the book.*)

KLESHCH. Oo, the grand madam! But you'll marry Abramka. It's all you've been waiting for.

KVASHNIA. Oh yes, of course! Naturally! What else? And there's you, driving your little wife there till she's half dead . . .

KLESHCH. Belt up, you old bitch, that's none of your business.

KVASHNIA. Ha! Can't take a spot of truth, eh!

BARON. There they go. Well, Nastya, where've you got to?
NASTYA (*without looking up*). Eh? . . . Oh, go away!

ANNA *puts her head out from under the canopy.*

ANNA. Oh God, the day's started! For pity's sake don't shout,
don't start rowing.
KLESHCH. She's whining again.
ANNA. Every single God's day the same! Can't you even let me
die in peace?
BUBNOV. Noise don't get in the way of death.

KVASHNIA *goes over to* ANNA.

KVASHNIA. How did you ever put up with such a useless animal,
girl?
ANNA. Leave off. Leave me be.
KVASHNIA. Well, well, there's a patient little martyr, then!
How's the chest now, any easier?
BARON. Kvashnia! Time to go to market!
KVASHNIA. Just coming. (*To* ANNA.) Why don't I give you some
nice hot dumplings, now?
ANNA. No, don't . . . Thank you. What's the point of me eating?
KVASHNIA. You just eat them, now. Something hot softens your
insides. I'll put them in a bowl and leave them here, then if you
feel like it you can have them. (*To* BARON.) Come on then, your
lordship. (*To* KLESHCH.) You – you're a nasty piece of work,
you are. (*She exits to the kitchen.*)
ANNA. (*coughs*). Lord . . .

The BARON *nudges the back of* NASTYA's *neck.*

BARON. Give it up, stupid girl.
NASTYA (*mutters*). Get away . . . I'm not hurting you.

The BARON *follows* KVASHNIA *into the kitchen, whistling.*
SATIN *props himself up on his bed.*

SATIN. Who was it beat me up last night?

BUBNOV. Does it make any difference?

SATIN. Maybe not. But why did they do it?

BUBNOV. Did you play cards?

SATIN. I did.

BUBNOV. That's why you got beaten, then.

SATIN. Bastards.

The ACTOR *sticks his head over the top of the stove.*

ACTOR. One of these times they do you in, they'll do you in for good.

SATIN. And you are an imbecile.

ACTOR. Why?

SATIN. Because you can't be done in more than once.

ACTOR (*after a pause*). I don't understand. Why can't you?

KLESHCH. You get yourself down off that stove and clear this place up. What do you think you're doing, fondling yourself up there?

ACTOR. Mind your own business.

KLESHCH. You wait till Vassilissa comes in, she'll soon learn you whose business it is.

ACTOR. Vassilissa can go to hell, it's the Baron's turn to clear up today. (*Shouts.*) Baron!

The BARON *comes out of the kitchen.*

BARON. I've no time for housework. I'm going to the market with Kvashnia.

ACTOR. You can go to Siberia if you like, it's nothing to me, but it's still your turn to sweep the floor. I'm not going to do other people's work for them.

BARON. May you be damned, then. Nastionka'll do the sweeping – Hey, Fatal Love, wake up! (*He snatches* NASTYA's *book away.*)

NASTYA (*getting up*). What d'you want? Give it here, you cheeky lout! Call yourself a gentleman!

BARON (*giving her the book*). Sweep the floor for me, Nastya, there's a good girl!

NASTYA (*going into the kitchen*). Oh, yeah, that's all I need.

KVASHNIA (*from the doorway, to the* BARON). You come along now, they'll get the floor swept without you. (*To* ACTOR.) Why don't you do as you're asked, it won't break your poor little back will it?

ACTOR. It's always me. Why is it always me?

> *The* BARON *comes out of the kitchen carrying a yoke hung with baskets in which there are earthenware pots, each covered with a cloth.*

BARON. Seems heavy today, somehow.

SATIN. Fat lot of good it did you, being born a baron.

KVASHNIA (*to* ACTOR). See you get that floor swept, now.

> *She exits into the passage, allowing the* BARON *to go through the door in front of her. The* ACTOR *climbs down from the stove.*

ACTOR. I oughtn't to breathe dust, it's bad for me. (*With pride.*) My organism is poisoned with alcohol.

SATIN. Organism . . . organon . . .

ANNA. Andrey Mitrich . . .

KLESHCH. What is it now?

ANNA. Kvashnia left some hot dumplings . . . You take them, you eat them.

> KLESHCH *goes over to her.*

KLESHCH. Won't you have some?

ANNA. I don't want any. Why should I eat? You're a working man, you must have something to eat.

KLESHCH. You scared? Don't be scared. Maybe you'll still . . .

ANNA. Go and eat the dumplings! I feel bad. I don't think it'll be long now.

KLESHCH (*walking away*). Never mind. Maybe you'll get up again. It happens sometimes . . .

> *He goes into the kitchen.*

ACTOR (*loudly, as if he is just waking up*). Yesterday at the clinic

the doctor said to me, 'Your organism,' he said, 'is completely
poisoned with alcohol'.

SATIN (*smiling*). Organon.

ACTOR (*firmly*). Not organon. Organism.

SATIN. Sycamore . . . sycambro . . .

ACTOR (*waving his hands dismissively*). Oh, nonsense! I'm serious,
I tell you. If my organism is poisoned it must be bad for me to
sweep the floor . . . breathe in all that dust . . .

SATIN. Microbiotins . . . ha!

ACTOR. What? What are you mumbling about?

SATIN. Words. Words. And then there's . . . trans-cend-dental-
istic!

BUBNOV. What's that, then?

SATIN. Don't know. Forgotten.

BUBNOV. Why say it, then?

SATIN. Because. I'm sick of all these everyday words. Sick of
them. I must have heard every one of them a thousand times.

ACTOR. There's a line in 'Hamlet' – 'Words, words, words'. It's
a good piece. I played the gravedigger.

KLESHCH *comes out of the kitchen.*

KLESHCH. When are you going to play with that broom?

ACTOR. Mind your own business. (*He strikes a pose, hand on
breast.*) 'Ophelia! Ah . . . remember me in thy orisons . . .'

*Offstage, in the distance, muffled sounds, shouting, a police
whistle.* KLESHCH *sits down to his work, scraping away with a
file.*

SATIN. I like . . . rare words, words you can't understand. When
I was young I had a job in a telegraph office . . . used to read
books . . . lots of books . . .

BUBNOV. So you were a telegraphist too, were you?

SATIN. I was . . . (*He gives a short laugh.*) There are some very
good books, you know . . . and lots of curious words. I was an
educated man, d'you know that?

BUBNOV. I've heard it a hundred times. Well, all right, so you were. Very important. And me, I had my own establishment – a master furrier, I was. My forearms were all yellow, from the dye, I used to dye the furs, and my hands and arms were so yellow, you know, right up to the elbow, I used to think I'd never get it washed off. Thought I'd die with yellow hands. And now here they are, look, same hands – just dirty. Yeah.

SATIN. Yes – well?

BUBNOV. Well – er – that's all.

SATIN. What are you trying to say?

BUBNOV. Just . . . thinking it out. It means, however much you paint yourself up on the outside, it all gets rubbed off . . . all gets rubbed off . . . hm.

SATIN. [I'm stiff. My bones ache.]

ACTOR (*sitting with his arms clasped round his knees*). Education . . . is bunk. What matters is talent. I knew an actor, he had to spell out his part syllable by syllable . . . could hardly read. But when he went out there and gave his performance, the whole theatre crackled and shook with excitement.

SATIN. Bubnov – let me have five kopeks.

BUBNOV. I've only got two.

ACTOR. What I say is, *talent* is what you need to be a star. And talent means believing in yourself, in your own strength . . .

SATIN. Give me five kopeks and I'll believe you're a talent, a star, a crocodile, a police inspector . . . Kleshch give us a five!

KLESHCH. Go to hell. There's too many of your sort here . . .

SATIN. No need for the abuse! I know you're cleaned out.

ANNA. Andrey Mitrich, I can't breathe, it hurts to breathe.

KLESHCH. What can I do about it?

BUBNOV. Open the door into the passage.

KLESHCH. Oh, fine. There's you, sitting up on your bed, and I'm down here on the floor. Change places, then you can open the door . . . I'm bloody freezing.

BUBNOV (*calmly*). I don't need to have it open. It's your wife that needs it.

KLESHCH (*gloomily*). Who cares who needs what?

SATIN. My head's splitting . . . Oooh! Why do people have to go about bashing each other on the head?

BUBNOV. They'll bash you on anything they can get hold of if you give them the chance. (*Gets up.*) Well, got to go and buy some thread. [What's happened to those landlords of ours today? Maybe they've up and died, at last.]

> BUBNOV *goes off.* ANNA *coughs;* SATIN *lies motionless, his hands behind his head. The* ACTOR *looks round unhappily, and goes over to* ANNA.

ACTOR. Feeling bad?

ANNA. Can't . . . breathe . . . in here.

ACTOR. Shall I take you out in the passage? Come on – up . . . up!

> *He helps her get up, throws a ragged garment over her shoulders, supports her out to the passage.*

Walk, dammit! I'm ill myself – poisoned with alcohol.

> KOSTYLIOV *appears in the doorway.*

KOSTYLIOV. Off for a walk, eh? Pretty little pair – the ram and his little ewe lamb!

ACTOR. Out of the way – can't you see we're invalids?

KOSTYLIOV. Of course, of course, come along then!

> KOSTYLIOV *sings something liturgical under his breath, looking round suspiciously, inclining his head on one side as if listening for something from Pepel's room.* KLESHCH *rattles his keys furiously and scrapes away with the file, furtively watching the landlord.*

KOSTYLIOV. Scrape-scraping, huh?

KLESHCH. What?

KOSTYLIOV. I said, you're *scraping*!

> *Pause.*

Ah – the – ugh – what was it I was going to ask? (*Fast, in a low voice.*) My wife wasn't here, huh?

KLESHCH. Haven't seen her.

KOSTYLIOV moves carefully over to the door to Pepel's room.

KOSTYLIOV. What a lot of space you've got out of me for your two roubles a month! A bed ... and there you are, sitting about ... h'm, yes, before God I'd call that five roubles worth of space! We'll have to slip a wee half rouble on you I can see ...

KLESHCH. Why not slip a noose round my neck and have done with it? You'll be dead soon, and there you're still dreaming about half roubles.

KOSTYLIOV. A noose? What would I do that for? Who'd gain from that? No, no, God's peace on you, man, you live on regardless to your heart's content. But I'll just put that half rouble on you, it'll buy some oil for the sanctuary lamp ... and my sacrifice will burn before the holy icon, my sacrifice will go up for me, in reparation for my sins, and for yours as well ... After all, you don't think about your sins for yourself. So there we are. Oh, Andriushka, you're a wicked man! Your wife's dying because of your wicked ways, and nobody loves you, nobody respects you, you just scrape, scrape away, upsetting everybody ...

KLESHCH (*shouting*). Did you come here just to bait me!

SATIN growls loudly.

KOSTYLIOV (*startled*). Oh, dear me, come now ... !

The ACTOR comes in from the passage.

ACTOR. I've settled your woman in the passage, wrapped her up ...

KOSTYLIOV. There's kindness, brother! That's good, you know, that'll be all on the reckoning for you.

ACTOR. When?

KOSTYLIOV. In the next world, little brother! Everything, all our deeds, all being reckoned up, for reward.

ACTOR. How about you rewarding me here for my 'kindness'?

KOSTYLIOV. How could I do that, now?

ACTOR. Knocking off half my debt.

KOSTYLIOV. He-he! Always joking, dear friend, always play-acting! As if you could compare goodness of heart with money! Goodness – goodness is above all other blessings. And your debt to me – that's still a *debt*! And so you're endebted to repay it. You must show kindness to your elders without looking for rewards.

ACTOR. Elders? You're an old leech!

He goes into the kitchen. KLESHCH *gets up and goes into the passage.*

KOSTYLIOV (*to* SATIN.) Scrape-scrape's taking himself off – he-he! He doesn't like me!

SATIN. Who does? Apart from . . . Satan?

KOSTYLIOV (*with a little laugh*). Oh, you and your abuse! And yet I love you all, I understand you, you're my fallen brothers, lost, good-for-nothing . . . (*Suddenly, quickly.*) Is Vasska in?

SATIN. Look and see.

KOSTYLIOV *goes over to the door and knocks.*

KOSTYLIOV. Vasska!

The ACTOR *appears in the kitchen door. He is chewing.*

PEPEL (*off*). Who's that?

KOSTYLIOV. It's me – me, Vasska.

PEPEL. What d'you want?

KOSTYLIOV (*moving away*). Open the door.

SATIN (*not looking at* KOSTYLIOV). He'll open it, and she'll be in there.

ACTOR *snorts.*

KOSTYLIOV (*anxiously, softly*). Eh? Who's in there? What . . . you what? . . .

SATIN. What? What – what? . . . You talking to me?

KOSTYLIOV. What did you say just then?

SATIN. Just talking to myself.

KOSTYLIOV. You watch it, brother! Watch you don't take your jokes too far. Yes. (*Knocks loudly on the door.*) Vasska!

PEPEL *opens the door of his room.*

PEPEL. Well? What d'you want now?

KOSTYLIOV (*peering into the room*). I – er – you see, I – er –

PEPEL. You brought the money, then?

KOSTYLIOV. There's something I've got to see you about . . .

PEPEL. Have you brought the money?

KOSTYLIOV. What money? Now wait a . . .

PEPEL. The money, the seven roubles. For the watch. Well?

KOSTYLIOV. What watch, Vasska? Oh, you mean . . .

PEPEL. Now you look here! I sold you a watch yesterday, in front of witnesses, for ten roubles, right? I've had three, so you just hand over the other seven! [What are you gawping at? Hanging about here disturbing people, and don't even know your own business!]

KOSTYLIOV. Sh – sh! Don't be angry now, Vasska. That watch is . . .

SATIN. Stolen.

KOSTYLIOV (*severely*). I don't accept stolen goods. How can you . . .

PEPEL *grabs him by the shoulders.*

PEPEL. Why d'you come down here, badgering me? What d'you want?

KOSTYLIOV. But . . . Oh, nothing, I'll go away . . . if you're so . . .

PEPEL. Bugger off and get the money, go on.

KOSTYLIOV. What coarse people, really! (*He exits, tut-tutting.*)

ACTOR. A comedy!

SATIN. Splendid! I like it!

PEPEL. What's he doing in here? What's he want?

SATIN (*laughing*). Don't you know? Looking for his wife, of course. Why don't you knock him off, Vasska?

PEPEL. Catch me messing my life up over a shit like that.

SATIN. You could do a neat little job . . . then – marry Vassilissa – be our landlord!

PEPEL. Perfect joy, yes. You lot'd piss away all my property in a bar, and me too, like as not, in my loving kindness. (*He sits down on a bed.*) Old bastard . . . woke me up . . . Oh! and I was having this great dream! I was fishing, and I hooked this enormous great carp, you know, the sort of carp you only get in dreams, and there I was, playing him, playing him, and, you know, scared the line would snap, and I had the landing net all ready . . . now, now, I thought, any moment now . . .

SATIN. That wasn't a carp, it was Vassilissa.

ACTOR. He hooked Vassilissa years ago.

PEPEL (*angrily*). Ah, go to hell – and take Vassilissa with you.

KLESHCH *comes in from the hall.*

KLESHCH. Bloody perishing out there.

ACTOR. [Why didn't you bring Anna in? She'll freeze.

KLESHCH. Natasha took her up to the kitchen with her.

ACTOR. The old man'll chuck her out.

KLESHCH *sits down to work.*

KLESHCH. Then Natasha'll bring her down here.]

SATIN. Vasska, give me five kopecks!

ACTOR (*to* SATIN). Five! Really! Vasska, give us twenty.

PEPEL. I'd best let you have it fast or you'll take me for a rouble . . . Here.

SATIN. Giblartarr! Oh, there's no one in the world better than a thief!

KLESHCH (*gloomily*). Money comes easy to them, they don't have
to work for it.

SATIN. Money comes easy to lots of folk, but it's not so easy to
part them from it. Work? Make it pleasant for me, I might start
working. I might, you know! When work's a pleasure, life's
worth while, when work's a duty, life's a trial. (*To the* ACTOR.)
Hey, Sardanapaulous, come on!

ACTOR. Come on then, Nebuchadnezor! Oh, I'm going to get as
drunk as – as forty thousand alcoholics!

SATIN *and the* ACTOR *go out.*

PEPEL. Well – (*yawns.*) How's your wife?

KLESHCH. Can't be long now . . .

Pause.

PEPEL. I watch you – scraping away . . . It's pointless.

KLESHCH. What else should I do?

PEPEL. Nothing.

KLESHCH. How'd I eat, then?

PEPEL. People live.

KLESHCH. This lot? People? What sort of *people* are they?
Ragbags, cacklebums, gutterscum . . . People! I'm a working
man . . . I feel ashamed just to look at them . . . I been working
since I was so high . . . Think I'm not going to get out of here?
I'll scramble out, don't you worry, if it tears my skin off of me
I'll scramble out . . . You wait . . . the wife'll die . . . six months,
I've lived here six months, feels like six years . . .

PEPEL. You're no better than anyone else here. You got no
business talking like that.

KLESHCH. No better –! People with no honour, no conscience
. . . !

PEPEL (*indifferently*). What do you want with honour and conscience? You can't put them on your feet instead of boots.
Honour and conscience! They're for the strong and powerful,
not for us.

Enter BUBNOV.

BUBNOV. Oooh. (*Shivers.*) I'm freezing.

PEPEL. Bubnov, you got a conscience?

BUBNOV. Eh? Conscience?

PEPEL. That's it.

BUBNOV. Conscience? Me? What for? I'm not rich.

PEPEL. What I was saying, see? It's the rich who can use honour and conscience, right? Kleshch here's been going on about us how we've none of us got any conscience.

BUBNOV. Why? Does he want to borrow some?

PEPEL. No, he's got plenty of his own, he says.

BUBNOV. So he's selling some? Well, he'll get no buyers in here. A few cardboard cartons, now, I might buy those – on tick, mind you.

PEPEL (*sententiously, to* KLESHCH). [You're a fool, Andriushka. You ought to talk to Satin – or the Baron – if you want to know about conscience.

KLESHCH. I got nothing to say to those two.

PEPEL. They're brainier than you, that's why. Even if they are drunkards.

BUBNOV. A brainy man who's on the booze
      Has a double stake to lose.

PEPEL. Satin says, everybody wants his neighbour to have a conscience, but nobody's got any use for one himself. And that's the truth.]

NATASHA *comes in, followed by* LUKA *with a stick in his hand, a bundle on his shoulder, a kettle and a tea-pot hung from his belt.*

LUKA. Good health to you, honest people.

PEPEL (*stroking his moustache*). A-ah, Natasha!

BUBNOV. Honest people, huh! – the spring before last, maybe.

NATASHA. Here's a new lodger.

LUKA. It's all one to me, I've as much respect for a scoundrel.

The way I see it, there's no such flea as a bad flea – they're all blackies, and all jumpies. Now, my dear, where do I fit myself in here?

NATASHA *points to the kitchen door.*

NATASHA. In there, grandpa.
LUKA. In she says and in I go. For an old man, wherever it's warm, that's home.

LUKA *goes off into the kitchen.*

PEPEL. That's an amusing little old ferret you've brought us, Natasha.
NATASHA. More amusing than you. Andrey – your wife's up in our kitchen with us, you come and fetch her soon, will you?
KLESHCH. All right, I'll come.
NATASHA. It wouldn't hurt you to show a bit of love, now. It can't be long, you know.
KLESHCH. I know.
NATASHA. You know! It's not enough to know, you must try to understand. It's frightening to die.
PEPEL. I'm not afraid of death.
NATASHA. Oh no, of course not! Ah, such a brave big man!
BUBNOV [(*whistles*). And this thread is rotten . . .
PEPEL. It's true. I'm not afraid. I could take death in my arms right now – this very minute. Take a knife, plunge it into my heart – I'll die without a murmur . . . in fact I'd die with joy if death came from such a pure hand.
NATASHA (*going off*). Ah, go and try it on somebody else!]
BUBNOV (*drawling*). And this old thread is rotten . . .
NATASHA (*at the door to the hall*). Don't forget your wife, Andrey.
KLESHCH. All right.

NATASHA *goes out.*

PEPEL. She's a good little maid.
BUBNOV. The lass is all right.

PEPEL. But why does she have to be like that with me – putting me down all the time? She's a lost cause here anyway.

BUBNOV. And you're the one'll lose it for her.

PEPEL. Why me? No, I'm really sorry for her.

BUBNOV. [Like the wolf's sorry for the lamb.

PEPEL. Don't talk cock! I . . . I feel really sorry for her. It's awful for a girl like that to live in a place like this. I can see that.]

KLESHCH. Wait till Vassilissa catches you talking to her.

BUBNOV. Vassilissa? Mm – yes – that one won't give up what's hers too easy. A fearsome woman.

> PEPEL *lies down on a bed.*

PEPEL. Ah, to hell with both of you! Prophetic pricks!

KLESHCH. Just wait and see, that's all.

> LUKA *is heard singing in the kitchen.*

LUKA. 'In the dark of the night with the path disappearing . . .'

KLESHCH (*going into the hall*). Hark at him bawling . . .

PEPEL. Oh, it's all so bloody boring! Why do I get so bored? You go on living and living and everything seems fine, then suddenly, pow! like catching a cold – you're bored.

BUBNOV. Bored, huh?

PEPEL. Stiff.

LUKA (*sings*). 'Oh the path disappearing behind and before . . .'

PEPEL. Hey, you! Old man!

LUKA (*looking through doorway*). Would that be me?

PEPEL. You. Don't sing.

LUKA (*coming in*). Don't you like it?

PEPEL. When someone sings well I like it.

LUKA. Do I sing badly?

PEPEL. That must be it.

LUKA. Well fancy that, now! And I really thought I sang well! It's always that way. A man thinks to himself, Aha, I'm really

doing well, and then, lo and behold! – nobody else is pleased
with him at all!

PEPEL (*laughing*). That's true enough!

BUBNOV. You say you're bored with everything, and there you
are, laughing.

PEPEL. What's that to you, brown owl?

LUKA. Who here is bored?

PEPEL. I am.

Enter the BARON.

LUKA. Fancy! And there in the kitchen a young lass sits, reading
a book and – weeping! Truly! Real tears flowing . . . I say to
her, what is it then, my dear, eh? and she says, Ah, she says,
it's sad! What's sad? I say and she says, Here, she says, in the
book. And so that's what she finds to busy herself with. That
must be out of boredom, too.

BARON. That one's a fool.

PEPEL. Baron, have you had your morning tea?

BARON. I have. Further. Further!

PEPEL. Would you like me to stand you – a little half bottle?

BARON. Naturally. Further!

PEPEL. Get down on all fours and bark like a dog.

BARON. Imbecile! What are you – my employer? Or just a drunk?

PEPEL. Oh, come on! Bark for me! It'll amuse me. You're a
nobleman. Time was when you didn't look on people like us as
human at all. And all that.

BARON. Yes. And further?

PEPEL. What more? Now I'm going to make you bark like a dog.
And you'll do it, won't you? You will.

BARON. All right, I will. Imbecile! What kind of satisfaction can
you get from that when I am perfectly aware that by now I have
become almost lower than you? You should have made me crawl
on all fours when I was still not yet your equal.

BUBNOV. He's right.

LUKA. I'd call that right.

BUBNOV. What's gone is gone. All that's left is candle-droppings. There's no lords-and-ladies here, all's been shucked off, nothing left but the naked man.

LUKA. So all are equal ... And were you really a baron, my dear?

BARON. Whatever's this? Who are you, pigwigeon?

LUKA (*laughing*). I've seen a count, and I've seen a prince, but this is the first time I've set eyes on a baron – and it has to be a mouldy one.

PEPEL (*laughing*). Baron! For a moment there you had me shamed.

BARON. Time you got smarter, Vasska.

LUKA. Dear, dear! (*Shakes his head.*) I look at you, brotherkins, and your life is ... Oh ... (*Shakes his head again.*)

BUBNOV. .... a life where you quake the minute you wake.

BARON. We've all lived better. True. Once upon a time I woke in the morning to hot coffee and cream. Cream – yes.

LUKA. And yet we're all still just – humans. Pretend how you like, wriggle how you like, we die as we're born – just humans. And it seems to me people are getting cleverer all the time, more interesting ... and though they live worse and worse, they all want something better ... A stubborn lot.

BARON. Who are you, old man? Where did you spring from?

LUKA. Me?

BARON. You're a pilgrim – a traveller?

LUKA. We're all travellers on this earth. I've heard tell even our earth is a traveller in the heavens.

BARON (*severely*). That is so. But what about a passport? Do you have one?

LUKA (*after a pause*). And are you a 'detective', then?

PEPEL (*joyfully*). Ah, that's a crafty one! [This time the Baron's walked into it.

BUBNOV. Uhu, it's the nobleman's turn now.]

BARON (*embarrassed*). Oh, come now! I was only joking, old one, I don't have any papers myself ...

BUBNOV. Liar.

BARON. Well, yes, I have *papers* – but they're none of them any good.

LUKA. That's the way it is with papers – none of them are any good.

PEPEL. Hey, Baron! You coming down for that drink?

BARON. I'm with you. Well, goodbye, old one. You're a rascal, you know that?

LUKA. Everything's possible, my dear.

PEPEL (*at the door*). Come on, then.

PEPEL *goes out, followed quickly by the* BARON.

LUKA. Was that one really a baron?

BUBNOV. Who knows? He was a gent, that's for sure. Even now, sometimes, he'll suddenly give you a glimpse of it . . . He's not lost the touch.

LUKA. Maybe being a gentleman is like having the smallpox – a man gets better, but the marks remain.

BUBNOV. He's all right. He just gives a little kick like that sometimes, the way he did about your papers.

ALYOSHKA *comes in, drunk, with his accordion in his hand. He's whistling.*

ALYOSHKA. Hey, you monsters of the deep . . . !

BUBNOV. [What are you yelling for?

ALYOSHKA. Oh! Sorry! Excuse me! As a man of manners . . .]

BUBNOV. Been on the booze again.

ALYOSHKA. Booze? On the house! You know that inspector Medyakin? He just threw me out of the police station. And make sure, he says, there's not even a whiff of you on the streets of this town! Uh-uh! (*Wags a finger reprovingly.*) Not a whiff! Now I – am a man – of character. And that boss of mine . . . *snarls* at me! And what is he, this . . . boss? Aargh! A mis-con-cep-tion! He's a drunkard, this boss! And I – I am the sort of man . . . who doesn't wish for a thing. I don't want *any*thing –

full stop! Come on, you can have me for twenty roubles – no. No. I don't want a thing.

NASTYA *comes in from the kitchen.*

Offer me a million – I *don't want* it! And for me, a man of character, to be bossed about by a drunk – I don't want that either. I don't want it.

NASTYA, *standing by the door, shakes her head as she looks at* ALYOSHKA.

LUKA (*good-naturedly*). You're in a proper muddle, aren't you, lad?

BUBNOV. All men are fools.

ALYOSHKA *lies down on the floor.*

ALYOSHKA. There you are. Eat me up! I don't want – a single thing! I tell you, I am a desperate man! Tell me this – who ... is better than me? Or – why ... am I any worse than anyone else? You see! And that Medyakin says, don't you go out on the streets or I'll bash you to ... smithereens! But I'm going! Oh, yes, I'm going! I'll lie down in the middle of the street ... run over me if you like ... I don't want a thing!

NASTYA. Poor silly kid – look at the state he's in!

ALYOSHKA *sees her, and kneels.*

ALYOSHKA. Miss! Mamzell. Parley francey? Weiner Shnitzel? Quanta costa? Che bella fräulein! – I've been drinking ...

NASTYA (*loud whisper*). Vassilissa!

VASSILISSA *opens the door quickly, speaks to* ALYOSHKA.

VASSILISSA. You here again?

ALYOSHKA. Ah – good day to you, madam! Please do come in!

VASSILISSA. I told you not to set foot in here again, you young puppy, and here you are ...

ALYOSHKA. Vassilissa Karpovna, wouldn't you like me ... to play you a funeral march?

VASSILISSA *gives him a shove on the shoulder.*

VASSILISSA. Get out!

ALYOSHKA *moves towards the door.*

ALYOSHKA. No – wait – don't be like that! The funeral march! I only just learnt it! A brand new piece! You mustn't be like that!
VASSILISSA. I'll give you *mustn't*! I'll set the whole street on you, you filthy blabbermouth! You're too young to go round yapping about me!
ALYOSHKA (*running out*). I'm going, I'm going!
VASSILISSA (*to* BUBNOV). You see he doesn't set foot in here again, understand?
BUBNOV. I'm not your watchdog.
VASSILISSA. I don't care who you are, you're living here on charity don't forget! How much do you owe me?
BUBNOV (*calmly*). Haven't counted.
VASSILISSA. You watch it, or I will!

ALYOSHKA *opens the door, shouts.*

ALYOSHKA. Vassilissa Kar-pov-na! I'm not af-RAID of You-ou! Not af-rai-aid!

He disappears. LUKA *laughs.*

VASSILISSA. And who might you be?
LUKA. A passer-by.
VASSILISSA. Spending the night, or staying?
LUKA. I'll see.
VASSILISSA. Passport.
LUKA. You'll get it.
VASSILISSA. Give it me now.
LUKA. I'll bring it – bring it to your very door.
VASSILISSA. [A passer-by, indeed! Pilferer would be more like it.
LUKA (*sighing*). Ah, you've an unkindly way with you, motherkin.]

VASSILISSA *goes over to the door into Pepel's room.*
ALYOSHKA *looks in through the kitchen door, whispers:*

ALYOSHKA. Psst! Has she gone?

VASSILISSA *rounds on him.*

VASSILISSA. You still here?!

ALYOSHKA *whistles, disappears;* NASTYA *and* LUKA *laugh.*

BUBNOV (*to* VASSILISSA). He's not there.
VASSILISSA. Who isn't?
BUBNOV. Vasska.
VASSILISSA. Who asked you?
BUBNOV. I see you looking round and about.
VASSILISSA. I'm looking to see if everything's in order, all right?
Why hasn't the place been swept yet? How often have I got to
tell you to keep the place clean?
BUBNOV. It's the actor's turn to sweep up.
VASSILISSA. I don't care whose turn it is! If those sanitary
inspectors come round and I'm fined, out you go – the lot of
you!
BUBNOV (*calmly*). Then what'll you live on?
VASSILISSA. It's got to be spotless – spotless! (*She goes into the
kitchen; to* NASTYA.) What are you hanging about here for?
Why are your eyes all swollen like that? Don't stand there like a
tree stump – sweep the floor! Have you seen Natasha? Has she
been in here?
NASTYA. I don't know. I haven't seen her.
VASSILISSA. Bubnov! Was my sister in here?
BUBNOV. Uhu. She brought him in.
VASSILISSA. Was that thing home?
BUBNOV. Vasska? Yes. But she was talking to Kleshch, Natasha
was.
VASSILISSA. Did I ask who she was talking to? Ugh! Filth
everywhere! Filthy! Pack of pigs, you are! See it's cleaned up,
you hear?

VASSILISSA *goes out quickly.*

BUBNOV. She's vicious, that one.

LUKA. A severious little ladybug.

NASTYA. Anyone'd get vicious, leading her life. Tie any living thing to a man like hers . . .

BUBNOV. She's not tied that tight.

LUKA. Does she always . . . explode like that?

BUBNOV. Always. She came to see her lover; you see, and he wasn't here . . .

LUKA. And that was an offence. Ah-ha. Dear me, all these different souls on this earth, all trying to order things the way they want, and frightening each other with all sorts of fears . . . and for all that, there's no order in life, nothing's clean-cut and pure.

BUBNOV. Order we want, brew it we can't. However, there's sweeping to be done. Nastya! Why don't you get on with it?

NASTYA. Oh, yes, of course! I'm your chambermaid, aren't I?

Pause

I'm going to get drunk today. Stinking drunk.

BUBNOV. Ah, well, of course, that's a serious business too.

LUKA. Why do you want to get drunk, lass? A while ago there you were, weeping. And now you say you want to get drunk!

NASTYA (*defiantly*). I'll get drunk – and then I'll have a cry again. That's all.

BUBNOV. It's not much.

LUKA. But what's the reason for it, my dear? You don't get blisters without bad boots, do you?

NASTYA *is silent, shaking her head.*

Well, well – (*He tut-tuts.*) – ah, people, people – what's to become of you? As for me, I might as well sweep up the floor for you – where's the broom?

BUBNOV. In the passage, behind the door.

LUKA *goes out into the passage.*

Nastionka!

NASTYA. What?

BUBNOV. Why did Vassilissa lay into Alyoshka like that?

NASTYA. He's been going around saying that Vasska's tired of her and would like to drop her and take up with Natasha instead. I'm getting out of here. Find myself another place.

BUBNOV. What? Where?

NASTYA. Anywhere. I'm sick of all this . . . I don't belong here.

BUBNOV (*calmly*). You don't belong anywhere. Nobody on earth belongs anywhere.

> NASTYA *shakes her head, goes out quietly into the hall. Enter* MEDVEDIEV, *followed by* LUKA *with the broom.*

MEDVEDIEV. I don't seem to know you.

LUKA. And the others – you know all of them?

MEDVEDIEV. It's my job to know everyone in my parish. And I certainly don't know you.

LUKA. That, uncle, is because the whole world hasn't quite been got into your parish – a mite's been left out in the cold.

> LUKA *goes out into the kitchen.* MEDVEDIEV *goes up to* BUBNOV.

MEDVEDIEV. My parish isn't all that big, it's true – but it's far worse than any of the big ones. A few minutes ago [– just before I came off duty,] I had to take that cobbler, Alyoshka, into the station. He was laying down in [the street, you know, laying there in] the middle of the street, playing that accordion of his and singing out I DON'T WANT ANYTHING, I DON'T WANT A SINGLE THING! [And there was all the traffic going past him, horses trotting along and everything,] he could have got run over or something! [He's wild, that boy!] Well, so I took him in. He likes to make a disturbance.

BUBNOV. Coming in for a game this evening?

MEDVEDIEV. Might as well – Mm – yes. What's Vasska up to?

BUBNOV. Nothing. Same as usual.

MEDVEDIEV. He's living all right, is he?

BUBNOV. Why not? He's allowed to live.

MEDVEDIEV (*doubtfully*). Don't know about that.

LUKA *passes through to the hall, carrying a bucket.*

Mm – yes . . . There's a lot of talk, you know . . . about Vasska. Have you heard?

BUBNOV. I hear quite a bit of talk.

MEDVEDIEV. About Vassilissa and . . . Haven't you noticed?

BUBNOV. Noticed what?

MEDVEDIEV. Oh . . . just – things . . . in general . . . Perhaps you know it all and you're lying? *Every*body knows! (*Severely.*) You mustn't lie, my friend.

BUBNOV. Why should I lie?

MEDVEDIEV. That's it. Why? Oh, the bastards! [They're all saying Vasska and Vassilissa, they say . . .] what's it got to do with me, I'm her uncle not her father, why laugh at me?

KVASHNIA *enters.*

That's the way people are these days, they'll laugh at anything . . . (*Sees* KVASHNIA.) Aah, there you are!

KVASHNIA. Ha – my precious police force! You know what, Bubnov! He was going on at me again, down at the market, about me marrying him!

BUBNOV. Do it. Why not? He's got a bit of money, and I'm sure he's still got plenty of juice in him.

MEDVEDIEV. Who, me? (*He chortles.*)

KVASHNIA. Listen, you looby, don't you touch me there, I tell you, not on my sore spot now! I been through that one, my pet. Getting married's like jumping through a hole in the ice for us poor women – you do it once and you remember it for the rest of your life.

MEDVEDIEV. Hold on now! Husbands aren't always the same, you know!

KVASHNIA. But I'm always the same. When my dear departed

husband finally went to his grave – may his soul never find rest –
I spent the whole day just sitting alone with my job, I tell you
I just couldn't believe my luck.

MEDVEDIEV. If your husband used to beat you for no good reason
you should have complained to the police.

KVASHNIA. I complained to God for eight years – he didn't help.

MEDVEDIEV. Wife-beating's prohibited now, there's a decent
severity and order in everything. Nobody can be beaten for
nothing, only for the sake of law and order.

LUKA *comes in, supporting* ANNA.

LUKA. There now, we've crawled our way in somehow . . . Deary
me, you shouldn't be out and about in your feebleness! Which
is your place?

ANNA *points to her bed.*

ANNA. Thank you, grandpa.

KVASHNIA. There's a married woman for you. Look at her!

LUKA. The little ladybug has an extremely feeble debilitution.
She was creeping along the passage, clutching the wall and
groaning . . . Why do you let her go out there by herself?

KVASHNIA. Ah, forgive us our wickedness, little father! Madam's
personal maid must have gone out for a walk.

LUKA. All right, laugh about it – but how can you abandon a soul
like that? Everybody, whatever he is, has his own worth.

MEDVEDIEV. Not enough surveillance! What if she died? There'd
be a lot of bother. Got to keep a watch on things.

LUKA. Very true, sergeant.

MEDVEDIEV. H'mm, yes . . . though I'm not – er – quite a
sergeant.

LUKA. Truly? Well, well, but your bearing is ever so sergeantic,
sir.

Noise and footsteps from the hall, muffled shouts.

MEDVEDIEV. Not another brawl?

BUBNOV. Sounds like it.

KVASHNIA. Best go and see.

MEDVEDIEV. Suppose I must – duty's duty. Why do people have to be separated when they start fighting? [They'd stop of their own accord, sooner or later.] After all, people get tired when they fight, so why not let them bash each other about to their heart's content, till they've had enough? [That way they'd fight less because they wouldn't forget what a real beating feels like . . .]

BUBNOV (*climbing down off the bed*). You go and tell your chief that . . .

KOSTYLIOV *flings open the door, shouting:*

KOSTYLIOV. Abram! . . . Quick! Vassilissa is . . . she's killing Natasha! Go on, quick!

KVASHNIA, MEDVEDIEV *and* BUBNOV *rush out.* LUKA *looks after them, shakes his head.*

ANNA. Oh God! Poor little Natasha.

LUKA. Who's fighting up there?

ANNA. Our landladies – sisters.

LUKA *goes over to* ANNA.

LUKA. What are they dividing up then?

ANNA. Oooh – you know – That's the way it is. They're both well fed, big healthy girls . . .

LUKA. What's your name?

ANNA. Anna. Look at you – you're just like my old father – just as gentle, just as tender . . .

LUKA. I've been well trampled, that's why I'm tender.

He gives a cackling laugh.

CURTAIN

Act Two

The same set as Act One. Evening.

On plank beds round the stove SATIN, BARON, KRIVOY ZOB *and* TARTAR *are playing cards.* KLESHCH *and the* ACTOR *are watching the game.* BUBNOV *is sitting on his plank bed playing draughts with* MEDVEDIEV. LUKA *is sitting on a stool beside* ANNA'S *bed. The dosshouse is lit by two lamps, one hanging on the wall beside the card-players, the other on* BUBNOV'S *bed.*

(KRIVOY ZOB. Bloody hell, they've done us again, Assan!)

TARTAR. [One . . . stay.]

(One more time, then finish.)

BUBNOV. Flopchin – sing!

(*He sings.*)

'Though the bright sun may be shining . . .'*

KRIVOY ZOB (*joining in*). 'My dungeon stays as dark as night.'

TARTAR (*to* SATIN). Shuffle! Shuffle 'em good! We know about you.

BUBNOV
KRIVOY ZOB (*together*). 'The prison guard stands by my window – oh – oh
And with his body steals my light.'

ANNA. Beatings. Curses. I've never known anything else. I haven't!

LUKA. Ah, little ladybug, don't be sad!

MEDVEDIEV. Where are you going with that? Careful, now!

BUBNOV. Aha! Right, right!

TARTAR *shakes his fist at* SATIN.

TARTAR. You try to hide card, [huh? I see you! You . . .]

* The full text of the song appears on page 90.

KRIVOY ZOB. Leave him, Assan. They'll outswindle us any case. Hey, Bubnov! [Sound off!]

KRIVOY ZOB *and* BUBNOV *sing.*

ANNA. I don't remember ever having enough to eat. Every bit of bread I've ever eaten I've shook over, been shaking all my life in case I was taking more'n my share . . . Gone about in rags all my life . . . all my rotten life. What did I do?

LUKA. Ah, childerkin! Tired, are you? Never mind.

ACTOR (*to* KRIVOY ZOB). The jack – you've got to play your jack, dammit!

BARON. Although we have a queen.

KLESHCH. They always win.

SATIN. It's become a habit.

MEDVEDIEV. And now – there's a king!

BUBNOV. Two can play at that . . .

ANNA. I'm going. Dying.

(KRIVOY ZOB. Hey, Assan, come on! One more time!)

KLESHCH (*to* TARTAR). Have some sense, Prince, don't go in again! Get out of the game I tell you!

ACTOR. Has he no mind of his own?

BARON. Careful now, Andriushka, or I'll put the evil eye on you!

TARTAR. Deal again! Pitcher keeps going to well and . . . pitcher break himself! Same as me.

KLESHCH, *shaking his head, goes over to* BUBNOV.

ANNA. And I keep thinking, Lord, Lord, surely I'm not going to be punished in the next world as well? Not there too, surely?

LUKA. There won't be anything at all. Lie still now and don't you worry a whit. [Nothing at all. You'll rest there. Bear up a bit longer.] Everybody has to bear his life, each in his own way.

LUKA *gets up and walks out quickly into the kitchen.*

BUBNOV (*sings*). 'Guard me, though I need no guarding –'
KRIVOY ZOB (*sings*). 'I can't hope to break this chain . . .'

BUBNOV

KRIVOY ZOB   (*sing together*).   'But stand aside from my window – oh – oh That I may see the sun again.'

TARTAR (*shouts*). Hey! You shove card up your sleeve!

BARON (*embarrassed*). Well, where would you like me to shove it – up your arse?

ACTOR (*firmly*). No, Prince, you're mistaken, no one would dream of . . .

TARTAR. I saw! Is cheat! No more play.

SATIN (*collecting the cards*). Oh, come off it, Assan. You know we're villains – so why play with us?

BARON. You lose forty 'pecks and make enough noise for three roubles . . . really, for a Prince . . . !

TARTAR (*angrily*). Must play honest!

SATIN. Whatever for?

TARTAR. How that, whatev' for?

SATIN. What I say – whatever for?

TARTAR. You don' know?

SATIN. I don't. Do you?

The TARTAR *spits furiously. They all laugh at him.*

KRIVOY ZOB (*amiably*). You are a prick, Assan! Don't you see, if they started to be honest they'd starve to death in three days.

TARTAR. Is nothing to me. I say man must live honest!

KRIVOY ZOB. Doesn't he keep on! Why don't we go and get some tea? Buben –

Sings.

'Oh you chain, you heavy mooring . . .'

BUBNOV (*sings*). 'Oh you cru-el iron bond . . .'

KRIVOY ZOB. Come on, Assanka!

He goes out singing.

'I can never shake nor break you-oo-oo.'

BUBNOV

KRIVOY ZOB   (*together*).   'And roam the sunlit world beyond.'

The TARTAR *shakes his fist at the* BARON *and follows his friend out.*

SATIN [(*to the* BARON, *laughing*). Well, your lowness, thou hast once again solemnly plonked thyself in the shit. An educated man, and can't even palm a card!

BARON (*shrugging*). God knows what happened.

ACTOR. No talent – not enough faith in yourself! Without that, nothing. No faith, no success – nothing!

MEDVEDIEV. I've got one king and . . . H'm. You've got two.

BUBNOV. Just one can survive, if his brain is alive. Go on. Move!

KLESHCH. You've lost, Abram Ivanich.

MEDVEDIEV. Mind your own business. Understand? And shut up!

SATIN. The winnings – fifty-three kopecks.

ACTOR. The three 'pecks for me . . . though come to think of it, what do I want three kopecks for?]

LUKA *comes out of the kitchen.*

LUKA. Well, did you take the Tartar? You'll be going for a drop of vodka now, then?

BARON. Come along with us.

SATIN. It'd be worth it, to see what you're like when you're drunk.

LUKA. No better than when I'm sober.

ACTOR. Come on, old one. I'll give you a few couplets.

LUKA. What are they?

ACTOR. You know – verses.

LUKA. Ah, *ve-erse*s! But what good are they to me, verses?

ACTOR. They can make you laugh. Or sad, sometimes.

SATIN. Come on, coupleteer. (*To* BARON.) You coming?

SATIN *exits with the* BARON.

ACTOR. You go on, I'll catch you up. Listen, old one, I'll give you some lines from a poem . . . I forget how it begins . . . H'm . . . forgotten . . . (*He rubs his forehead.*)

BUBNOV. That's it! There goes your king. Your move.

MEDVEDIEV. Dammit, he went wrong there somewhere . . .

ACTOR. Before my organism was poisoned with alcohol, old one, I had an excellent memory. But it's finished now, everything's finished for me. I used to declaim that poem with enormous success . . . to tumultuous applause! You wouldn't know what applause means . . . it's like vodka, brother! I'd make my entrance, take up my pose . . . (*Poses.*) So! I'd stand there, so, and . . . (*He is silent.*) Don't remember any of it. Not a word. Just – don't remember. And it was the poem I loved the best . . . Is that bad, old one?

LUKA. What could be good about it, if you've forgotten something you loved? Your whole soul goes into what you love.

ACTOR. I've drunk my soul away, old one. Done myself in. Done for – and why? Because I had no faith. I'm finished.

LUKA. Why? Cure yourself! They can cure you of drunkenness now, you know. Cure you free of charge, brotherkin! There's a sort of clinic been built for drunkards, to cure them, you know, for free. They've allowed that a drunk is a human soul same as anyone else, and they're actually pleased if he wants to get himself cured! Well there you are then! You go!

ACTOR (*thoughtfully*). Go? Where? Where is it?

LUKA. Oh, it's in a town – now, what is it? It's called . . . something-or-other. Oh, I'll see you get the name all right. Now, here's what you do. First you prepare yourself. Try and keep away from it . . . get a grip on yourself, and – bear with it. Then one day you'll be cured and begin to live all over again . . . it's good, brotherkin, all-over-again is good! Just make up your mind . . . two easy steps . . .

ACTOR (*smiling*). All-over-again, eh? Right from the start. That's good, yes. All over again? (*Laughs.*) Oh . . . yes! I can? I can, can't I?

LUKA. Why not? A human soul can do anything – if he really wants to.

ACTOR (*suddenly, as if waking up*). You're a comic, aren't you? Goodbye for now – (*He whistles.*) Goodbye, old one!

ANNA. Grandpa!
LUKA. What is it, little one?
ANNA. Talk to me.

   LUKA *crosses to her bed.*

LUKA. All right, let's talk together, then.

   KLESHCH *looks round, goes silently over to his wife, looks at
   her, and makes movements with his hands as if he wants to say
   something.*

What, brother?
KLESHCH (*in a low voice*). Nothing.

   *He slowly goes over to the door into the hall, stands in front of it
   for a few moments, then goes out.*

LUKA (*looking after* KLESHCH). It's painful for that little husband
   of yours.
ANNA. I'm past caring about him.
LUKA. Did he beat you?
ANNA. Did he ever! It was him started me on the coughing.
BUBNOV. My wife . . . had a lover. Very handy at draughts, he
   was, the villain.
MEDVEDIEV. H'mm.
ANNA. Grandpa . . . talk to me, dear. I feel so sick.
LUKA. It's nothing. It's only – death's beginnings, little pigeon.
   It's nothing, my dear. Just hope. You'll do a little dying, that's
   all, and then you'll be wrapped in the long peace . . . [nothing
   more asked of you, nothing to fear! Silence, peaceness, you
   just lie.] Death – quietens everything, she strokes us to sleep
   . . . Blest in their rest are the dead, they say, and that's true,
   my dear, for where is there here for a soul to rest?

   Enter PEPEL. *He is slightly drunk, dishevelled, and gloomy.
   He sits down on the plank bed by the door and remains silent
   and motionless.*

ANNA. But how will it be there? More miseries?

LUKA. Nothing! There'll be nothing! Believe me. Peaceness –
and nothing else. You'll be called before the Lord and they'll
say, Lord, look here on your servant Anna . . .

MEDVEDIEV. How do you know what they're going to say there?
You . . .

> PEPEL *looks up at the sound of* MEDVEDIEV'*s voice and starts
> listening.*

LUKA. It must be – that I know, sergeant.

MEDVEDIEV (*conciliatory*). H'm, yes. Well, that's your line, I
suppose . . . (*mumbles*) . . . not . . . exactly . . . uh . . . sergeant.

BUBNOV. Double jump!

MEDVEDIEV. Oh, you . . . May you be . . . !

LUKA. And the Lord's eyes will stroke you, and he'll say, I know
this Anna! Now, He'll say, you take this soul, Anna, into
paradise, let her be soothed . . . I know how hard her life's been,
she's tired, let Anna rest . . .

ANNA (*sighing*). Oh grandpa, good grandpa . . . if only it could be
like that! if only there'll be peace . . . not to feel anything . . .

LUKA. You won't. There'll be nothing – believe that! Die with
joy, without fear . . . for I tell you, death to us is like a mother to
her little children.

ANNA. But perhaps . . . perhaps . . . I'll get better?

LUKA (*with a short laugh*). What for? More 'miseries'?

ANNA (*grunts*). Just a . . . a little more . . . if only I could live . . .
just a little bit more! If there's not going to be any torment
there, I could bear it here for a while . . . I could!

LUKA. There'll be nothing! Just . . .

PEPEL (*loudly*). True! Or perhaps – not true!

ANNA (*fearfully*). Oh God!

LUKA. Hello, handsome.

MEDVEDIEV. Who's shouting?

> PEPEL *goes up to* MEDVEDIEV.

PEPEL. I am. So what?

MEDVEDIEV. You got no business shouting, that's what. A soul should behave peaceably.

PEPEL. Ah, you dumb ox! Fine big uncle you are, aren't you?

LUKA (*quietly, to* PEPEL). Listen, don't shout. The little woman here's dying, her lips are already tasting the loam. Don't disturb her.

PEPEL. Oh, dutiful respects, grandpa. You're a fine old feller too. I can see that. You lie well, that's the thing – tell pleasant little tales. You lie on regardless, then – there's none too much in this world that's pleasant.

BUBNOV. Is she really dying, that one?

LUKA. Doesn't look as if she's joking.

BUBNOV. Then she'll stop coughing. She was always coughing – very unrestful it was. Double jump.

MEDVEDIEV. Oh, you should be shot through the heart!

PEPEL. Abram.

MEDVEDIEV. I'm not Abram to you.

PEPEL. Abrashka – is Natasha poorly?

MEDVEDIEV. None of your business.

PEPEL. No, tell me – did Vassilissa knock her about badly?

MEDVEDIEV. That's none of your business either. It's family business. Who do you think you are?

PEPEL. Whoever I think I am, I could make sure none of your lot saw Natasha again if I wanted to.

MEDVEDIEV (*stops playing*). You ... What did you say? What are you talking about? My youngest niece could ... you ... you're just a thief!

PEPEL. A thief, perhaps – but not one you've caught.

MEDVEDIEV. You wait! I'll catch you soon enough!

PEPEL. You'll be sorry if you do, you and your whole tribe. You don't imagine I'd keep my mouth shut in front of the magistrate, do you? You can't keep a fox in a box! Who started you thieving, they'll ask, who gave you the tip-offs? Mishka Kostyliov and his wife! And who received the stolen goods? Mishka Kostyliov and his wife!

MEDVEDIEV. Liar. They'd never believe you.

PEPEL. They'd believe me – because it's true. Oh, and I'll drag you into it too . . . Ha! I'll destroy the whole rotten pack of you, you wait and see!

MEDVEDIEV (*at a loss*). Liar! And – and – liar! And – and – what harm have I ever done you? You're like a mad dog!

PEPEL. What good have you ever done me?

LUKA. Ah-a.

MEDVEDIEV (*to* LUKA). What are you grunting about, what's it got to do with you? This is family business.

BUBNOV (*to* LUKA). [Leave it. They're not tying nooses for our necks.

LUKA (*serenely*). Didn't say a word. All I do say is, if someone has done nothing good to a person, then they've done bad.

MEDVEDIEV (*not understanding*). That's it, you see, all of us here, now, we know each other and . . .] Who are you, anyway?

He snorts angrily, goes out quickly.

LUKA. He's lost his temper, that official gentleman. Tsk-tsk! I can see your affairs are in a muddle, brothers.

PEPEL. He's gone off to snivel to Vassilissa.

BUBNOV. You're acting like a fool, Vasska. You keep your end up all right – but you watch it. [Boldness is all very well when you're off to the woods with a girl to gather mushrooms – but it won't do here, on your own doorstep.] That lot'll rip your guts out in no time.

PEPEL. We-e-ell – as a matter of fact, no. You can't take a man from Yaroslavl with your bare hands. When it's war, we fight.

LUKA. But it's true, brotherkin – you should get away from this place.

PEPEL. Where to? Got anything in mind?

LUKA. Take yourself off to Siberia.

PEPEL. Ha! No, if it's going to be Siberia, I'll wait to be sent at Government expense.

LUKA. No, listen, you take yourself off there! [You could find a road for yourself there, you're just the kind of man they need there.

PEPEL. My road was laid down for me long ago. My father spent his whole life in jail, and booked the same berth for me. Even when I was a kid I was called thief and son-of-a-thief.]

LUKA. It's a good part of the world, though, Siberia, a golden part. Anyone strong and in his right mind can make himself a nice snug bed there, and grow like a cucumber.

PEPEL. Why do you lie all the time, old one?

LUKA. Eh?

PEPEL. Gone deaf suddenly? Why do you lie, I said?

LUKA. Lie? When've I lied?

PEPEL. All the time. You say it's wonderful here, wonderful there, and you're lying. What for?

LUKA. Just believe me. You trot off and see for yourself. You'll thank me. What are you hanging around here for? And why are you so keen on the truth? Think now – the truth is a blade that can turn.

PEPEL. It's all one to me. If the blade turns, it turns.

LUKA. Ah, you're all dreams! What's the point of letting oneself be killed?

BUBNOV. What are you two drivelling on about? I don't understand. What truth do you want, Vasska, and what for? You know the truth about yourself and so does everyone else.

PEPEL. Wait, stop croaking, Bubnov. Just let him tell me ... Listen, old one – does God exist?

LUKA *smiles, says nothing.*

BUBNOV. People's lives are just chips on the water – the house gets built, but the chips float away.

PEPEL. Well? Does he? Go on.

LUKA (*in a low voice*). If you believe – he does. If you don't – he doesn't. Whatever you believe in, exists.

PEPEL *gazes intently at* LUKA, *in silence, astonished.*

BUBNOV. I'm going for some tea. Come on – hey!
LUKA (*to* PEPEL). What are you staring at?
PEPEL. So that . . . wait a minute . . . that means . . .
BUBNOV. Ah well, I'll go by myself.

BUBNOV *goes towards the door, where he is met by* VASSILISSA.

PEPEL. What you mean is . . .
VASSILISSA (*to* BUBNOV). Is Nastya here?
BUBNOV. No.

BUBNOV *goes out.*

PEPEL. Oh, you're here.

VASSILISSA *goes over to* ANNA.

VASSILISSA. Still alive?
LUKA. Don't disturb her.
VASSILISSA. What are you hanging about here for?
LUKA. I can go if necessary.

VASSILISSA *goes over to the door of* PEPEL's *room.*

VASSILISSA. Vasska. There's something I want to talk to you
about.

LUKA *goes to the hall door, opens it, then shuts it loudly again.
He then stealthily climbs on to a bed and from there on to the
top of the stove.* VASSILISSA *calls from Pepel's room.*

Vasska! Come here.
PEPEL. I won't. Don't want to.
VASSILISSA. Why not? Why are you so cross?
PEPEL. I'm tired of it – sick of all the fuss.
VASSILISSA. And tired of me?
PEPEL. Tired of you, too.

VASSILISSA *pulls her shawl tightly about her shoulders, pressing
her hands to her chest. She goes over to* ANNA's *bed, looks carefully behind the canopy, and goes back to* PEPEL.

Go on, then.

VASSILISSA. What can I say? You can't be forced to love . . . and it's not my way to beg for kindness . . . Thank you for the truth.

PEPEL. What truth?

VASSILISSA. That you're tired of me . . . or perhaps you aren't?

PEPEL looks at her in silence. She moves up to him.

Why are you staring? Don't you recognize me?

PEPEL (*sighs*). You're a fine-looking woman, Vassilissa.

She puts her arm around his neck, but he shrugs it off with a movement of his shoulder.

But you never came near my heart. I lived with you and all that . . . but I never cared for you.

VASSILISSA (*quietly*). I see. So . . .

PEPEL. So we've got nothing to talk about. Nothing. Just leave me alone.

VASSILISSA. Is there someone else?

PEPEL. None of your business. If there was, I wouldn't use you as a go-between.

VASSILISSA (*significantly*). You'd be wrong about that. I might be the very person who could do it.

PEPEL (*suspiciously*). What d'you mean?

VASSILISSA. You know – why pretend? Vasska, I'm a straight-forward person . . . (*Quietly*). I won't try to hide it – you've hurt me . . . for no reason at all . . . as if you'd lashed at me with a whip. Saying you loved me and then suddenly . . .

PEPEL. Not suddenly. For a long time I've . . . There's no heart in you, woman! A woman must have heart in her! We're wild animals, we need . . . we have to be trained, and you – what kind of training did you give me?

VASSILISSA. That's all past and done. I know we're none of us our own masters. You don't love me any more – all right, that's it.

PEPEL. Well, that's the end, then. We're parting peacefully, without a fuss, and that's fine.

VASSILISSA. No, wait, I'm not finished. When – when I was with you – I was always – waiting. Hoping you'd help me to get out of this – cesspit, get away from my husband, my uncle, this whole rotten way of life. [I don't know, but maybe it wasn't really you I loved at all, Vasska; maybe it was just this – this hope, this idea – I was loving and seeing in you.] Do you understand? I was waiting for you to drag me out of here.

PEPEL. I'm not a pair of pincers. No, what I thought was, what with you being so smart . . . because you are smart, Vassilissa, I grant you that, you're clever . . .

VASSILISSA (*leaning close to him*). Vasska! We could – help each other . . . Couldn't we?

PEPEL. How?

VASSILISSA (*quietly, insistently*). My sister – you like her, don't you?

PEPEL. That's why you knock her about so savagely, isn't it? You watch it, Vassilissa! Keep your hands off her!

VASSILISSA. [Wait, please,] don't get angry. It could all be arranged quietly, smoothly. You want to marry Natasha – all right, I'll give you money as well! Silver roubles . . . three hundred of them! And more, when I can save more!

PEPEL (*moving away*). Hey, now, hold on! What d'you mean, what are you getting at?

VASSILISSA. Free me . . . from that man. Take that . . . noose off my neck!

PEPEL (*whistles softly*). So that's it! Oh, yes! That's a smart bit of thinking, all right! Your husband to his grave, your lover to jail, and yourself . . .

VASSILISSA. No, Vasska! No need for jail! You could get friends to do it – and even if it was you, who'd ever find out? Think of Natasha – think! And the money . . . you'll be able to get away somewhere . . . and I'll be free for ever . . . and Natasha would be better off away from me . . . I can't look at her without burning with hatred, and then I can't stop myself, I torture the poor girl, because of you, beat her, beat her until I'm weeping with pity for her . . . but I keep on beating her. And I'll go on beating her.

PEPEL. You're a savage. [It's nothing to boast about.]

VASSILISSA. [Not boasting – speaking the truth.] Think, Vasska! Twice now you've been to jail because of my husband, because of his greed! [He fastened on me like a leech – he's been sucking my blood for four years now. What sort of a husband is he?] And he bullies Natasha, [ridicules her,] tells her she's a beggar! He's poison for everyone, he's just poison.

PEPEL. Cunning, the way you twist your snares.

VASSILISSA. I've been straight enough with you – only a fool could get me wrong.

   KOSTYLIOV *comes in carefully and steals forward.*

PEPEL. You'd better go.

VASSILISSA. Think, Vasska! (*She sees her husband.*) What is it? Come for me, huh?

   PEPEL *starts, and looks wildly at* KOSTYLIOV.

KOSTYLIOV. It's me, yes! And here you are, alone together, eh? Talking together?

   He suddenly stamps his foot and squeals loudly.

You slut! You selfish tramp!

   He is alarmed by his own shouting, which the others meet with silence, remaining motionless.

God forgive me, Vassilissa, you've led me into sin again! I've been looking for you everywhere . . . (*Shrieking again.*) It's bedtime! And you've forgotten to put oil in the votive lamps! Oh, you tramp, you sow!

   He makes a dismissive downward movement of his trembling hands. VASSILISSA *walks slowly over to the door, looking back at* PEPEL.

PEPEL (*to* KOSTYLIOV). Get away from here.

KOSTYLIOV (*shouting*). It's my house! Get away yourself, thief!

PEPEL (*in a stifled voice*). Watch out, Mishka.

KOSTYLIOV. Don't you dare ... I'll ... You'll ...

> PEPEL *grabs him by the scruff of the neck and shakes him. Loud scuffling noises and howling yawns start from on top of the stove.* PEPEL *lets go of* KOSTYLIOV, *who scampers out with a cry.* PEPEL *jumps up on to a bed.*

PEPEL. Who's that? Who's up there?

> LUKA *sticks out his head.*

LUKA. Eh?

PEPEL. You.

LUKA (*calmly*). None other. Oh, Lord Jesus Christ!

> PEPEL *closes the door, looks for a bolt but can't find one.*

PEPEL. Bastards! Come down, old one.

LUKA (*drawling*). I'm coming.

PEPEL (*roughly*). What were you doing up on the stove?

LUKA. Where else should I have gone?

PEPEL. But ... you went outside ... ?

LUKA. Brotherkin, outside's too cold for an old man like me.

PEPEL. You heard?

LUKA. I heard. Couldn't help it. I'm not deaf. [Ah, luck's on your side, young one, luck is really on your side.

PEPEL (*suspiciously*). What d'you mean? What luck?

LUKA. Me, up on the stove.]

PEPEL. Why did you suddenly start making all that noise?

LUKA. Started getting too hot ... [your orphan luck again.] And then, I was figuring, what if the young one made a mistake ...? What if he accidentally strangled that old man?

PEPEL. I could've, too. I hate him.

LUKA. Isn't it natural? Nothing more easy! Mistakes like that happen all the time.

PEPEL (*smiling*). Maybe you made a mistake yourself, once?

LUKA. Young one, you listen to what I got to say: that woman, you keep her away from you. (*He wags his finger.*) Don't you let her come anywhere near you! She'll harry her husband to his grave neater than you can. Don't you listen to the witch. Look – see how bald I am? And why? Because of women of all sorts, I must have known more of these women than maybe there were hairs on my head and I tell you, that Vassilissa, she's worse than a scyllaritdis!

PEPEL. I don't know. Do I say thank you? Or are you another?

LUKA. Don't say anything. You won't say better than me. Just hear me – the one you want here, take her arm, and quick march, away from here! Get away from here, right away!

PEPEL (*gloomily*). How can you tell about people – which are good and which are bad? I don't understand a thing.

LUKA. There's nothing to understand. Men live every which way, according as his heart is set so a man lives, good today, bad tomorrow ... If that lass has got severiously into your heart, get away with her and have done. Otherwise, go alone. You're young, you've time enough to acquire a woman.

PEPEL *takes* LUKA *by the shoulders.*

PEPEL. No, why are you giving me all this ...?

LUKA. Wait – let go. I must have a peek at Anna. She was breathing a bit heavy, somehow ...

He goes over to ANNA'*s bed, opens the canopy, looks in, and touches her with his hand.* PEPEL *watches thoughtfully, with a puzzled air.*

All-merciful Jesus Christ, receive with mercy the newly departed soul of thy servant Anna!

PEPEL (*quietly*). Is she dead?

Without going nearer, he stretches up to look over to the bed.

LUKA. She's suffered her way out of it. Where's that old whinger of hers?

PEPEL. Drinking, most likely.

LUKA. Must tell him.

PEPEL (*shuddering*). I don't like dead bodies.

LUKA (*going to door*). Why should you? It's the living you should like, the living!

PEPEL. I'm coming with you.

LUKA. Afraid?

PEPEL. Don't like it.

They go out hurriedly. The place is quiet and deserted. Beyond the hall door can be heard muffled sounds – it's not clear what they are. Then the ACTOR *enters. He stops on the threshold with the door open, hanging on to the door frame. Shouts:*

ACTOR. Old one! Hey! Where are you? I've remembered! Listen!

Swaying, he takes two steps forward, strikes a pose, and declaims:

'If the world, my friends, should fail to find
The road to sacred truth,
All honour to that fool whose mind
With golden dreams wraps round mankind.'

NATASHA *appears in the doorway behind the* ACTOR.

Old one! Listen!
'If tomorrow, my friends, the sun should seem
Too tired to light the earth,
Some madman's mind would dream a dream
More dazzling than the sun's own beam.'

NATASHA (*laughing*). You scarecrow, you're drunk again!

The ACTOR *turns round to her.*

ACTOR. Aha, you're there, are you? But where's the old one – the nice little old man? Looks as if there's no one here. Well, Natasha – goodbye! Yes – farewell!

NATASHA comes further in.

NATASHA. You haven't said hello yet, and now you're saying goodbye.

The ACTOR *bars her way.*

ACTOR. I'm leaving – going away! Spring will arrive – and find me gone!

NATASHA. Let me by. Where are you off to?

ACTOR. To look for a town . . . to get myself cured . . . You should go away too – Ophelia! get thee to a nunnery! And somewhere in the world, you see, there's a clinic, a clinic for organisms! For drunken organisms! Oh yes, a fabulous clinic, with . . . marble . . . yes, marble floors! Light, clean and everything – food and everything – free! And . . . and marble floors, yes. And I shall find it, I shall get myself cured, and once again I shall be . . . all-over-again . . . I am on the road to rebirth, as – ah – King – ah – Lear said! On the stage, Natasha, my name was Sverchkov-Zavolzhshky – no one knows that, Natasha, no one! I don't have any name at all here. Can you imagine how that hurts – to lose your name? Even dogs have names.

NATASHA walks carefully round the ACTOR, *stops beside* ANNA's *bed, looks in.*

No name – no man.

NATASHA. Look – Oh my dear, she has done it; she has died!

ACTOR (*shaking his head*). No-o-o . . .

NATASHA (*stepping back*). Before God – look!

BUBNOV (*in the doorway*). Look at what?

NATASHA. Anna. She's dead.

BUBNOV. Stopped her coughing, has she?

He goes over to ANNA's *bed, looks at her, and then goes to his own place.*

Better tell Kleshch. That's his business.

ACTOR. I'll go and . . . and tell him that . . . that she's lost her name.

The ACTOR *goes out.*

NATASHA (*in the middle of the room*). That's how it'll be with me some day . . . end up . . . in a basement . . . beaten . . . smashed . . .

BUBNOV [(*spreading rags out on his bed*). What? What are you mumbling about?

NATASHA. Just . . . talking to myself.

BUBNOV. Waiting for Vasska, are you? You be careful – he'll be the end of you, that one.

NATASHA. I'd as soon it was him as another.

BUBNOV (*lying down*). Well, it's your own business.

NATASHA. She's better off dead, of course, but it's sad all the same . . .] Lord, what was it for – a life like that?

BUBNOV. It's the same for everyone – they're born, they live for a bit, then they die. I shall die. So will you. What's sad about it?

Enter LUKA, *the* TARTAR, KRIVOY ZOB *and* KLESHCH. KLESHCH *comes in behind the others, slowly, his shoulders hunched.*

NATASHA. Ssssh! Anna . . .

KRIVOY ZOB. Yeah, we heard. Lord have mercy on her.

TARTAR (*to* KLESHCH). Humped out there must be – pulled out in hall. Here not possible dead person, here live persons sleep.

KLESHCH (*quietly*). We'll take her out.

They all go over to the bed. KLESHCH *looks at his wife over the others' shoulders.*

KRIVOY ZOB (*to the* TARTAR). You afraid she'll smell? She won't, you know. She was all dried up already before she died.

NATASHA. Oh God, if only there was a drop of pity somewhere . . . if only one of you had a single kind word! Oh, you . . . !

LUKA. Don't take on burdens, little one. It's nothing. How can they – how can any of us pity the dead when we can't even pity ourselves?

BUBNOV (*yawning*). And then again, death don't wince at words. An illness might, but not death.

TARTAR (*stepping back*). Police must . . .

KRIVOY ZOB. Police – right! Kleshch! You told the police?

KLESHCH. No. And there's the burial . . . I've only got forty kopecks.

KRIVOY ZOB. For a thing like this, you got to borrow. [Or p'raps we'll have a whip round – five from one, so much from another . . .] But you got to tell the police, quickly, else they'll start saying you killed her or something . . .

He goes over to the TARTAR's *bed and prepares to lie down beside him.* NATASHA *goes over to* BUBNOV's *bed.*

NATASHA. And now I shall dream about her. I always dream about dead people . . . I'm scared to go back alone – it's dark in the hall.

LUKA (*watching her*). You watch out for the living, that's all I say.

NATASHA. See me back, grandpa.

LUKA. Come on with you, then, I'll see you back.

They go out together. Pause.

KRIVOY ZOB. Oh-oh-ooh! Assan! It'll be spring soon, man! Warm living again! They're already mending their ploughs in the villages, all set for turning the soil again . . . Aah! . . . ye-e-es! And how about us, Assan . . .? Jesus, fucking Mahommed's asleep already.

BUBNOV. Tartars love to sleep.

KLESHCH *stands in the middle of the room, gazing stupidly in front of him.*

KLESHCH. What do I do now?

KRIVOY ZOB. Lie down and sleep. What else?

KLESHCH (*quietly*). But . . . she . . . How can I?

Nobody answers him. Enter SATIN *and the* ACTOR.

ACTOR (*shouts*). Hey, old one! Here, my faithful Kent!

SATIN. Here comes our brave explorer! Ho-ho!

ACTOR. It's all settled and decided, old one! Where's that town of yours? Where are you?

SATIN. Off to Phantasmagoria! Crap! – The old one lied to you, there's nothing! No town, no people, no clinic – nothing!

ACTOR. Liar!

TARTAR (*jumping up*). Where landlord? I go landlord! Not possible sleep, not possible pay rent ... Dead persons, drunk persons ...

Muttering, he goes out quickly. SATIN *whistles after him.*

BUBNOV (*sleepily*). Lie down, you lot, don't make such a row ... night ... must sleep.

ACTOR. Aha, yes ... here ... the dead! 'Let the dead past bury its dead.' A p-poem by ... Béranger.*

SATIN (*shouts*). The dead can't hear! The dead can't feel! Shout – howl – the dead can't hear!

LUKA *appears in the doorway.*

CURTAIN

* The Actor actually quotes a poem of Pushkin's which is very well known in Russia: 'Daddy, daddy, our nets have dragged in a dead man!' But unless the quotation is a familiar one, the misattribution to Béranger is lost. Hence our borrowing from Sir Walter Scott.

Act Three

'The Waste Land' – a patch of yard littered with all kinds of rubbish and overgrown with weeds. At the back is a high brick wall which blocks out the sky. Elder bushes grow beside it. To the right, the dark wooden wall of some outbuilding – a barn or a stable. To the left, the grey wall – with its few remaining patches of stucco – of the building of which KOSTYLIOV's *dosshouse is the cellar. It stands at an angle, so that the back corner comes almost into the middle of the patch, forming a narrow passage between this corner and the red brick wall. There are two windows in the grey wall, one level with the ground, the other about five feet higher and nearer the brick wall. Against this wall lie wide, low sledges, their runners uppermost, and some planks, about nine feet in length. To the right by the wall, lies a heap of old boards and joists.*

Evening. The sun is setting, casting a reddish glow on the brick wall. It is early spring, and the snow has recently melted. There are no buds yet on the black elder twigs.

On a log NATASHA *and* NASTYA *are seated side by side.* LUKA *and the* BARON *are sitting on a sledge, and* KLESHCH *is lying on the pile of wood to the right. In the ground level window can be seen* BUBNOV's *face.* NASTYA, *with her eyes closed, speaks in a sing-song voice, shaking her head in time to her words.*

NASTYA. And so, at dead of night, into the garden he came, to the summer-house, as had been arranged between us. I had long been awaiting him there, trembling with fear and grief. He too was trembling all over and as white as a sheet, and there . . . in his hands . . . a revolverer!

> NASTASHA *is chewing sunflower seeds, breaking off the husks with her teeth and spitting them out.*

NATASHA. It's right, then, what they say, they are a wild lot, those students!

NASTYA. And in a fearful voice he says to me, 'Ah, my precious love, my pearl without price!'

BUBNOV. Ho, ho! Without price!

BARON. One moment! If you don't like the story don't listen, but don't interrupt the recitation. Further!

NASTYA. 'My sweetest love,' he says. 'My parents,' he says, 'will not give their consent to our marriage, and,' he says, 'they say they will curse me for all eternity because of my love for you. On which account,' he says, 'I am obliged to take my life.' And he had this revolverer, an enormous great thing it was and loaded with ten bullets. 'Farewell!' he says, 'gentle friend of my heart! I have taken an irreversal decision, for I cannot possibly live without you.' And I answered him, 'Oh, my never to be forgotten friend, Raoul . . .'

BUBNOV (*astonished*). What? Growl?

BARON (*laughing*). But, Nastya, last time it was Gaston!

NASTYA (*jumping up*). Shut up . . . you . . . you mangy dogs! How could you ever understand *love* – true love? And that's what mine was – *true*! (*To the* BARON.) You – you're nothing! Supposed to be an educated man, supposed to have drunk coffee in bed with cream in it . . .

LUKA. Now now, you two, wait, wai-ai-ait! (*Drawling the word out soothingly.*) Don't interfere. 'Tisn't the word that matters. But why has the word been spoken, that's what matters. Tell on, then, girl.

BUBNOV. Go on, then. Paint your feathers, draggletail.

BARON. Yes, yes! Further!

NATASHA. [Don't you listen to them, Nastya. They don't mean a thing. They're just jealous, that's all. They've got nothing to tell, themselves.]

NASTYA *sits down.*

NASTYA. Shan't tell any more. Don't want to. If they're not going to believe me, if they're going to laugh at me . . .

Suddenly breaking off, NASTYA *is quiet for a few seconds and then, closing her eyes again, she starts to talk passionately and loudly, her hand beating time to her words, as if she is listening to music in the distance.*

And so I answered him, 'Oh light of my life! heart of my heart! No more could I possibly live in this world without you, for I love you quite insanely, and ever will I love you while my heart beats within my breast! But,' says I, 'do not, oh do not take your own young life, for your dear parents so badly need you to live, you who are their only joy! No, no, rather leave me, forget me, rather let me perish with grief over the loss of you who are my whole life . . . I am alone in the world . . . let me be . . . forsaken . . . doesn't matter . . . I'm no good . . . nothing . . . I'm nothing . . . there's nothing here for me . . . nothing . . . '

NASTYA *covers her face with her hands and cries silently.* NATASHA *turns away from* NASTYA, *says quietly:*

NATASHA. Don't cry. Don't!

LUKA, *smiling, is stroking* NASTYA's *hair.*

BUBNOV (*laughing loudly*). Oh, isn't she the bloody limit, though?
BARON (*also laughing*). Hey, grandpa, you don't think it's all true, do you? She got it all out of that book – *Fatal Love*! It's a lot of nonsense! Don't waste your time on her!
NATASHA. What's it got to do with you? Shut up, can't you? Just because you're feebleminded yourself you . . .
NASTYA (*furious*). You – you – you're lost – empty – you're . . . what happened to your soul?

LUKA *takes* NASTYA *by the hand.*

LUKA. Come away, my dear. Pay no heed. Calm down now. I understand, I believe. It's your truth, not theirs. If you believe you've known true love, then you have, you have! [But don't be angry with him, you live with him, you mustn't quarrel with him. Maybe . . . he was only laughing . . . because he's jealous. Maybe he never had anything real happen to him, nothing at all!] Come away now!

NASTYA (*pressing her hands to her breast*).   Before God, Grandpa, it *did* happen, it all really happened! He was a student, a French student, called Gaston, and he had a little black beard and he – he went about in – in patent-lacquered boots . . . and – may I be struck down if I lie – he *loved* me, he loved me so much!

LUKA. I know. Never mind, I believe you. And patent-lacquered boots, eh? Fancy that! And you loved him too . . .?

They disappear round the corner.

BARON. Really, how stupid she is, that girl! Kind, perhaps, but unbearably stupid!

BUBNOV. Funny how people can get so fond of lying. She goes on as if she was always up in front of the magistrate. It's a fact!

NATASHA. It's obvious lies are more pleasant than the truth. I too . . .

BARON. Well? You too what? Further!

NATASHA. Well I . . . daydream . . . imagine things and . . . wait.

BARON. For what?

NATASHA (*smiling bashfully*). Just . . . well, I think, tomorrow, perhaps tomorrow someone will come, somebody . . . special will come. Or else, maybe, something will happen, that's never happened before. I wait – I've been waiting a long time, I'm always waiting, and of course, really and truly, what is there to wait for?

Pause.

BARON (*with a mocking smile*). Nothing. There's nothing to wait for. I'm not waiting for anything. Everything's already happened. It's over, finished! All right – further!

NATASHA. Or sometimes I think, tomorrow . . . perhaps to-morrow I'll suddenly die! And that makes me feel . . . all shivery. Summer's a good time for imagining about death, there's thunderstorms in summer, there's always a chance of death, when there's a thunderstorm.

BARON. You don't have much of a life, do you? That sister of yours – my God, she's vicious!

NATASHA. Who does have much of a life? As far as I can see it's bad for everyone.

Up to now KLESHCH *has been motionless and has taken no part in the conversation. Now he starts up.*

KLESHCH. Everyone? That's a lie! It's not bad for everyone! If it was, all right, that'd be the way of things, and it wouldn't all be such a bloody insult!

BUBNOV. Who got his teeth in you then? Yelping like that!

KLESHCH *lies down again, grumbling to himself.*

BARON. Suppose I'd better go and make my peace with Nastionka . . . if one doesn't go and make up one can't even get the price of a drink out of her . . .

BUBNOV. H'm . . . people do love telling lies, though . . . You can understand it with Nastya, she's used to painting her face, and she'd like to paint her soul as well, dab a bit of rouge on her soul. But what about the others – look at Luka, for instance, he's always telling lies and he gets nothing out of it. And he's an old man, that one. What does he do it for?

BARON (*with a smile, going out*). Everyone in the world's got a grey little soul – we'd all like to touch them up a bit.

LUKA *reappears from around the corner.*

LUKA. Why do you nag at the poor girl, sir? You should leave her be, let her weep away and amuse herself, she only does it for her own pleasure. What harm does it do you?

BARON. It's stupid, old one, and it's a bore. Today it's Raoul, tomorrow Gaston, and it's always the same stupid rubbish! Anyhow, I'm going to make it up with her.

The BARON *goes off.*

LUKA. Off you go then, and be gentle with her. It never does any harm to be gentle with a person.

NATASHA. You're kind, grandpa. Why are you so kind?

LUKA. Kind, am I? Well, all right, yes, if you say so.

From over the red wall come soft sounds of an accordion, and someone singing.

Somebody has to be kind after all, my dear. People need pity. Didn't Christ pity us all, and tell us to pity each other? I can tell you, it's good when you take pity on someone in time! For instance – I was once working as caretaker in a villa outside Tomsk. Belonged to an engineer. Right. Now this villa stood all alone in the forest – very lonely spot it was too! Winter in Siberia. And there I was, alone in the villa. All fine and good. But then, one day . . . there's this noise! Someone trying to climb in!

NATASHA. Thieves?

LUKA. Just that. So there they were, climbing in. I picked up a gun, and out I went. Looked round. Two of them there were, trying to open up a window – so busy working away at it they never even saw me. So I shouted. 'Hey! You! Get away from there!' They turned round – and come straight at me with an axe. 'Stop!' I warned them, 'Or I'll shoot!' And I kept moving the gun, now on one, now on the other. And down they went, down on their knees, begging me to let them go. Then I – well, I lost my temper. You know, because of the axe. 'I told you to go,' I said, 'and instead you come at me like limbs of Satan. So now,' I said, 'You over there, you break off that branch of twigs!' So he broke off the branch. 'And you,' I said, 'you lie down there, face down. Right. Now you – whip him!' And they did as I told them, and gave each other a whipping. And when the whipping was done they said . . . grandpa, they said, for the love of Christ, they said, give us a crust of bread! We haven't had a bite since we started out . . . There's thieves for you, my dear! (*He laughs.*) There's coming at you with an axe! Yes, good little fellers they were, the pair of them. [You should've asked me for bread straight off, I told them, but they said, Ah, we've had enough of that, asking and asking and nobody giving a crumb, it's insulting to a man . . .] And so they stayed with me the whole winter. [One of them, Stepan, he'd take the gun and go off hunting. The other one, Yakov, he was always sick, coughing all the time. So there we were, the three of us, looking after the villa.] When spring came it was, 'Goodbye, grandpa!' and off they went, making tracks back to Russia.

NATASHA. Were they on the run? Convicts?

LUKA. Just that. They'd run away from a penal colony. [Good little fellers they were.] But if I hadn't taken pity on them, they'd have maybe come back and killed me or something, and then it would have been the courts again, and prison again, and Siberia . . . and what's the sense in it all? Prison doesn't teach a man to be good, no more does Siberia. Only another poor soul can do that. It's true. One soul can teach good to another soul. It's simple.

Pause.

BUBNOV. H'm. Well, me, I can't tell lies. What's the point, anyway? The way I see it, let's have the whole truth coming out just as it is. Why shy away from it?

KLESHCH *again suddenly jumps up as if he'd been scalded, shouting.*

KLESHCH. Truth! What truth? Where's the truth! Here . . . (*He pulls at the rags he's wearing.*) There's the truth for you! Got no work . . . no strength left . . . there's the truth. No shelter, no place to go, might as well lie down and die, that's it, that's the truth of it. Shit! – what's the good of it to me, the truth? – it's shit! Let me get my head out and breathe! What have I done wrong, to be given the truth! Ah, Christ, living, living's just bloody impossible. And that's it. That's the truth of it.

BUBNOV. Whew! The devil's really nipped his arse this time!

LUKA. Lord Jesus! Listen, my dear, you . . .

KLESHCH (*trembling with excitement*). You and your *truth*! You just want to make everyone feel good, you old fool! Well, I'll tell you, I hate every last one of you, and as for the truth, may it be damned to hell. Got that? Well, just you get it!

KLESHCH *runs off round the corner, glancing back as he goes.*

LUKA (*tut-tuts, shaking his head*). Tsk-tsk! Fancy getting so excited! Where's he run off to now?

NATASHA. You'd think he'd gone off his head.

BUBNOV. What a performance! [He could have been on the stage.] It happens like that with him. He's not used to being alive yet.

PEPEL *comes slowly round the corner.*

PEPEL. Greetings, all. Well, Luka, you old rascal – still telling stories?

LUKA. You should've been here just now. Poor soul was shouting his head off.

PEPEL. Kleshch, you mean? What's up with him now? He was running like a scalded cat.

LUKA. When something gets too close to your heart – you run.

PEPEL. I don't like him. He's too proud, proud and bitter. (*Imitating* KLESHCH.) 'I'm a working man . . .' – as if he was any better than the rest of us. [All right, work, if that's what you like, but it's nothing to be proud about. If you're going to judge by work, horses are better than any man . . . slave all day, and never say a word.] Natasha. Your people at home?

NATASHA. They've gone to the cemetery . . . Then they were going to evening service.

PEPEL. Ah, that's it. I saw you were free for once.

LUKA (*thoughtfully, to* BUBNOV). Look, what you were saying, about the whole truth . . . you know, truth isn't always the right medicine for a man, you can't always cure a sick soul with the truth. For instance, here's a case . . . I knew this man who believed in the land of the righteous . . .

BUBNOV. The *what*?

LUKA. The virtuous land. There must be a virtuous country somewhere in the world, he said, a place where a special kind of people go to live, good people, who respect each other and help each other, just like that, quite simply . . . and all's fine and lovely amongst them. And so this man was all ready to go off and search for the virtuous land. He was a poor man, lived a hard life, but whenever things got so bad for him that he might just as well lie down and die, he'd never lose heart, he'd just smile to himself and he'd say, 'It's nothing, I can bear it, I'll just hang on a bit longer and then I'll be away, away from all this, away to the virtuous land.' It was his one joy, the thought of that land.

PEPEL. Well? Did he go?

BUBNOV. Go where? Ho-ho!

LUKA. And then one day – all this happened in Siberia – this exile arrived. A scientist, he was. And he'd brought with him all his books and his plans, had this scientist, and his maps and all manner of learned things. So this man says to the scientist, 'would you be so good,' he says, 'as to show me where the land of the virtuous lies, and how I can find my way there?' So the scientist straightway opens up his books, and he looks . . . but the land of the virtuous was nowhere to be found! All was correct, every country in the world was shown, everything there in its proper place . . . but among them, no virtuous land!

PEPEL (*quietly*). What? Nowhere at all?

> BUBNOV *laughs loudly*.

NATASHA. No, wait. Go on, grandpa.

LUKA. Well – this man just didn't believe it. 'It must be there,' he says, 'you go on and take a better look, because otherwise,' he says, 'if they don't show where the virtuous land is, all your

books and maps are completely worthless!' The scientist was
very offended. 'My maps,' he says, 'are exact and true, and
there is no land of the virtuous anywhere there at all!' Well, the
man got very angry when he heard this. 'What!' he says, 'here
I've lived and suffered and endured all this time, believing that
there is, and now your maps make out that there isn't! I've been
robbed!' he says to the scientist, 'Oh you swine,' he says, 'you're
a crook not a scientist!' And with that he fetched the scientist
a clout across the ear, and then another across the other. (LUKA
is silent for a moment.) Then he went home and hanged himself.

They are all silent. LUKA, *smiling, looks at* PEPEL *and* NAT-
ASHA.

PEPEL (*quietly*). Mother of God – that's not a very cheerful story.
NATASHA. He couldn't bear being cheated . . .
BUBNOV (*glumly*). It's all just – stories.
PEPEL. We-e-ell – so much for the virtuous land. Turns out there
isn't one.
NATASHA. It's sad . . . poor man.
BUBNOV. It's all just make believe. Go on, then – ho-ho! – the
virtuous land! That's the place to go! Ho-ho-ho!

BUBNOV *disappears from the window.* LUKA *shakes his head
in that direction.*

LUKA. He's laughing – oh well. (*Nods in direction of* BUBNOV's
window.) Hey-ho! – live richly, my friends! I'll be leaving you
soon.
PEPEL. Where are you off to now?
LUKA. To Little Russia. Hear they've discovered a new religion
there, must go and have a look. Must go, yes. People are always
searching, always asking for . . . something better. God give
them patience.
PEPEL. You think they'll find it?
LUKA. They're human – they'll find it. He who seeks, finds. He
who wants strongly enough, gets.

NATASHA. If only they would find something – think up something – better.

LUKA. They'll think it up. Only – we have to help, my dear. We have to respect them.

NATASHA. How could I help? I'm helpless myself.

PEPEL (*resolutely*). Natasha – I – I've spoken to you about this before, and I'm going to again – now, in front of him. He knows . . . all about it. Natasha – come away with me.

NATASHA. Where? Round the prison yards?

PEPEL. I told you, I'll give up thieving! I will, before God, I'll give it up! I've said I will, and I will. I can read and write – I'll get work. The old man here told me I should get myself to Siberia of my own free will – let's go there together, eh? You don't think I'm not sick of the kind of life I lead here, do you? Oh, Natasha, I know it all, I'm not blind! [Of course I say to myself, what about all those people who steal lots more than I do, and still have everyone looking up to them . . . but it doesn't help, that isn't the point.] Mind you – I'm not sorry about anything, and I still don't believe in conscience – but I do know this: I've got to live different somehow, got to live better, got to live somehow so I can have a bit of respect for myself.

LUKA. I'd call that right, my dear. [God grant it and Christ aid it! A man's got to respect himself and that's the truth of it.]

PEPEL. I've been a thief since I was that high. Vasska the thief – everyone always called me that – Vasska the thief's son, Vasska the thief. [So all right then, if that's the way it is – I'm a thief! You see –] maybe I'm only a thief because nobody ever thought to call me different – out of spite, sort of. Natasha – you could call me . . . something different. Well?

NATASHA (*sadly*). Somehow I can't believe any . . . words . . . today. I feel uneasy, my heart feels heavy – as if I was expecting something. I wish you hadn't started talking about all that today.

PEPEL. When, then? It's not the first time I've talked about it . . .

NATASHA. Why should I go with you, anyway? I don't love you –

well, not all that much . . . occasionally, perhaps, I quite like you, but other times it makes me sick to look at you, so I can't love you, can I? – [because people, when they love, can't see anything bad in the person they love. And I can.]

PEPEL. You'll come to love me, I promise! I'll teach you to! [Oh, Natasha, you only have to agree . . .! I've been watching you for over a year now and I know you . . .] you're good – very firm with yourself – reliable – and – and . . . I've come to love you very much.

VASSILISSA, *in her best clothes, appears at the window, and stands by the jamb, listening.*

NATASHA. So – you've come to love me. And what about my sister.

PEPEL (*embarrassed*). Well, what about her? There's plenty of her sort around . . .

LUKA. Never you mind old history, my dear. If a man can't get bread he'll eat pigswill . . . if there's really no bread at all. Forget all that.

PEPEL (*morosely*). Have a heart, Natasha – my life's been bare enough, God knows. There's not much joy in living like a wolf, with a criminal record and your passport marked . . . it's like drowning in a bog, wherever you step you go deeper in, whatever you grab at comes away in your hands, it's all stinking rotten . . . Your sister, I thought she was . . . turned out she was rotten too. If she hadn't been so bloody greedy . . . I'd have done anything for her . . . if she could have been mine, just for me, not for . . . but, no, she was after more than me, she was after money, and freedom – yeah! freedom to whore about all over town! No, she could never be any help to me . . . But you, Natasha, you're like a young fir tree – if a man clings to you, you may prick his hands but you hold up firm.

LUKA. And I tell you too, marry him, girl, get in behind him! He's all right, this lad, he's a good one. Only you got to keep reminding him, often, that he's a good one, so he won't go forgetting it! Just you tell him now and then, 'Vasska, you're a good man, you know – and don't you forget it!' And think, my dear – where else can you ever go? Your sister's a vicious beast, and her husband – [well, there aren't any words I'd want to waste on that one . . . And this life here, all this – where could it ever take you? And this lad is strong . . .]

NATASHA. No, there's nowhere to go. I know that, I've thought that too. It's just – I don't trust anyone . . . But it's true – there's no way I can go . . .

PEPEL. There's only one road. But I won't let you take that one. I'd rather kill you.

NATASHA [(*smiling*). There. I'm not even your wife yet, and you're talking about killing me already.

PEPEL (*embracing her*). Stop it, Natasha! All the same, I would . . .]

NATASHA (*pressing close to him*). There's . . . just one thing . . . I must say . . . and, Vasska, I say this before God! – the very first time you hit me, or – or – hurt me . . . any way at all . . . I swear I won't spare my own life, I – I'll either hang myself or – or . . .

PEPEL. May my arm wither, if I ever touch you!

LUKA. Don't you worry, my dear – trust him! He needs you more than you need him.

VASSILISSA (*from the window*). So there they are – the happy couple! For richer, for . . . poorer . . .

NATASHA. Oh my God, they're back! They saw! Oh, Vasska . . .!

PEPEL. What are you scared of? Nobody'll dare touch you now.

VASSILISSA. You needn't worry about him, Natasha, he won't beat you. He can't beat a woman any more than he can love one . . . I should know!

LUKA (*softly*). Poisonous woman. Viper.

VASSILISSA. He's only big with words.

KOSTYLIOV (*coming out*). Natasha! What do you think you're doing, you idle tramp! Gossip-mongering, eh? Complaining about your family? Yes, and with the samovar not ready and the table not laid, eh?

NATASHA (*going out*). You said you wanted to go to church . . .

KOSTYLIOV. What we do's none of your business, you should be attending to your own business, doing what you were told to do!

PEPEL. Pack that in! She's not your servant any more . . . Natasha, don't go, don't you do anything!

NATASHA. It's too soon for you to start giving me orders.

PEPEL (*to* KOSTYLIOV). That's enough! You've been trampling on her long enough. She's mine now.

KOSTYLIOV. You-ou-ours? (*Drawled mockingly.*) When did you buy her? How much did you pay?

> VASSILISSA *laughs loudly.*

LUKA. Vasska! Get away from here!

PEPEL. You – you watch out! You can laugh now – watch out you don't end weeping!

VASSILISSA. Ooh, how terrifying! Ooh, I am scared!

LUKA. Vasska, get away! Can't you see she's just goading you on, trying to get you mad – don't you understand?

PEPEL. Yes – aha! – yes! But she's got it all wrong! (*To* VASSILISSA.) You and your filth! What you want isn't going to happen, see!

VASSILISSA. What I don't want isn't going to happen either, Vasska!

PEPEL (*shaking his fist at her*). We'll see about that!

> PEPEL *exits.*

VASSILISSA (*disappearing from window*). I'll arrange a nice little wedding for you.

KOSTYLIOV (*going up to* LUKA). Well then, old one?

LUKA. Nothing then, old one.

KOSTYLIOV. So. You're going, I hear?

LUKA. It's time.

KOSTYLIOV. Where to?

LUKA. Where my eyes lead me.

KOSTYLIOV. Tramping, in other words. It doesn't suit you to stay in one place, then?

LUKA. A stone that never moves, they say, kills the grass it lies on.

KOSTYLIOV. That's for stones. But humans should live in one place, it's not right for people to live like cockroaches, crawling off every which way whenever they want. A man must root himself in his place, not go traipsing aimlessly about the face of the earth.

LUKA. What if there's a place for a man wherever he goes?

KOSTYLIOV. Then he's a tramp, a waster, useless! There must be some service come out of everyone, some work . . .

LUKA. So you say.

KOSTYLIOV. Yes, I do! Now, a pilgrim, a palmer – he's different, a strange man, not like other people at all . . . if he's truly seeking for something, knows something, has found out something or other . . . which no one else needs to know . . . well, so maybe he's found out the truth somehow, all right, but not every truth needs to be known, that's certain, so let him keep it to himself, keep quiet about it! If he's a true palmer, I mean, he keeps his silence . . . or . . . or he speaks so nobody can understand him . . . and he's not after anything, he doesn't interfere with anything, doesn't go stirring people up when he's not been asked to! It's not his business how other people live, his business is pursuing the paths of righteousness . . . he should live in forests . . . thickets . . . out of sight! And not disturb anybody, or judge anybody, no, but just pray . . . pray for everyone, for all the sins of all the world, for my sins and your sins, for everybody's sins! Yes! That's why he flees from worldly vanities, yes, in order to pray! And that's it.

Pause.

But you . . . what sort of a palmer are you? You haven't even got any papers. A decent person must have a purseport, all decent people have their purseport papers, oh yes!

LUKA. There are people – and there are human beings.

KOSTYLIOV. Don't start being clever! I don't need riddles from you, I'm just as intelligent as you are! What d'you mean, people and human beings?

LUKA. Where's the riddle? [I only say, some ground's good for sowing – what you sow, sprouts. And some ground's bad. That's all.

KOSTYLIOV. Well? What's the point of that?]

LUKA. Take you, for instance – if the Lord God himself said, 'Mikhail, be human' – well, even that wouldn't do any good – such as you are, so you'd remain.

KOSTYLIOV (*grunts menacingly*). . . . and do you know that my wife's uncle is a police officer, and if I . . .

VASSILISSA (*coming in*). Mikhail Ivanich, the tea is ready.

KOSTYLIOV (*to* LUKA). Now listen, you . . . you get out of here! Clear right out of these lodgings!

VASSILISSA. Yes, just you clear off, old one! Your tongue's a sight too long – and anyway, how do we know you're not on the run from somewhere?

KOSTYLIOV. I want you out of here today, understand? Otherwise I'll . . . well, you watch out!

LUKA. You'll call uncle? Call uncle, then, tell him you've caught a runaway. You never know, uncle might get a reward . . . three kopecks or so.

BUBNOV (*appearing at the window*). Hello, what's being sold out here? Three kopecks for what?

LUKA. They're threatening to sell me.

VASSILISSA (*to* KOSTYLIOV). Come on.

BUBNOV. For three kopecks? You be careful, old one. They'd sell you for one kopeck.

KOSTYLIOV (*to* BUBNOV). You . . . came popping out there like a goblin out of the hearth!

VASSILISSA (*leaving*). The world seems to be full of stupid people. Every kind of crook you can imagine.

LUKA. Enjoy your tea.

VASSILISSA (*turning*). Hold your tongue, you poisonous toad-stool!

VASSILISSA *and* KOSTYLIOV *go out.*

LUKA. Tonight . . . I shall leave.

BUBNOV. It's the best way. It's always best to leave in time.

LUKA. I'd say that's true.

BUBNOV. I know it. I probably missed a spell in Siberia by leaving in time.

LUKA. Is that so?

BUBNOV. It's the truth. It was like this – my wife had got herself mixed up with my master-furrier – first-class furrier he was, too, you should've seen the way he'd dye a dog-skin to turn it into racoon . . . or . . . or cat-skins into kangaroos, muskrats, whatever you like . . . Oh, he was a real craftsman! Well, so my wife gets herself mixed up with him, and there they were, thick as thieves the pair of them, and it wasn't going to take much for them to decide to poison me, or shuffle me out of the world some way or other. I took to beating my wife. Then the furrier took to beating me – vicious old fighter he was, too, one time he pulled out half my beard and broke one of my ribs. So I turned nasty too. One day I whacked my wife over the head with an iron scraper . . . and altogether there was a fine old war getting going between us. But no good was going to come of it, I could see that – they were getting the best of it. So one day I thought, right, well I'll have to kill the wife. Had a good hard think about that for a while . . . Then I saw sense, and came away.

LUKA. That was the best way. Let them go on turning cats into kangaroos.

BUBNOV. Only thing was, the workshop went to the wife of course, and I was left – as you see. Though, to be honest, I'd only have drunk the business away. I'm a drinker, you see.

LUKA. A drinker? A-ah.

BUBNOV. Terrible drinker. Once I start swilling it, I go on till I'm

soaked, nothing left but a skinful of vodka . . . I'm lazy, too.
Terrible . . . the way I hate work.

Enter SATIN *and the* ACTOR, *arguing.*

SATIN. Rubbish! You're not going anywhere, it's just the drink
talking! Hey, old one! What's all this hot air you've been
pumping into this fag-end?

ACTOR. Liar! I am going! Grandpa, tell him he's lying! I'm
going. I worked today – swept the street – didn't touch a drop
of vodka! How about that, then? Look at this. (*Jingles coins.*)
Thirty pretty 'pecks – and I'm sober!

SATIN. Ridiculous, that's what it is. Give 'em here, I'll drink
them for you . . . or lay them on a card.

ACTOR. Get away! They're towards my journey.

LUKA (*to* SATIN). Why do you keep trying to sap his strength?

SATIN. 'Tell me, Oh, Sorcerer, beloved of the gods, What will
befall me on my weary way?' Brother, I have been wiped out,
picked clean, every last 'peck. All is not yet lost for the world,
grandpa, while there's niftier cardsharpers in it than me.

LUKA. When you're merry, Konstantin, you're good company.

BUBNOV. Actor! Come over here.

The ACTOR *goes over to the window and squats on his haunches
in front of* BUBNOV. *They talk in low voices.*

SATIN. When I was young, brother – yes, I was really good
company then! It's good to think back on it – Oh, I was a ball
of fire! Dance splendidly, acted, loved to make people laugh . . .
It was good, all that.

LUKA. How did you come to lose your way?

SATIN. Nosey old greybeard, aren't you? There's nothing you
wouldn't like to know. What for?

LUKA. I like to understand . . . why people do what they do. I
look at you and . . . don't understand. You're a fine manly
fellow, Konstantin . . . clever . . . no fool, anyway . . . and
yet . . .

SATIN. Prison, grandpa. I spent four years and seven months in prison. After prison – there's no way up.

LUKA. A-ha. What were you in for?

SATIN. For a louse. Killed a louse in a fit of rage. It was in prison I learned to play cards.

LUKA. And you killed him because of some woman.

SATIN. Because of my sister . . . and that's enough, now. I don't like being questioned. And it was all a long time ago . . . nine years . . . my sister died nine years ago . . . she was a wonderful little creature, that sister of mine.

LUKA. You bear up well under life. And there was that locksmith a while back – you should have heard him howling, oh dear, oh dear!

SATIN. Kleshch?

LUKA. That's him. He was yelling, 'there's no work, there's no nothing!'

SATIN. He'll get used to it. What should I do with myself, I wonder?

LUKA (*softly*). Look. He's coming back.

Enter KLESHCH *slowly, his head bowed.*

SATIN. Well, widower, why've you got your snout in the dust? What's on your mind?

KLESHCH. I'm thinking . . . trying to think . . . what to do. My tools are all gone. The funeral ate up everything.

SATIN. I'll give you some good advice: don't do a thing. Just . . . be a burden on the world.

KLESHCH. You can talk like that . . . I've got my pride in front of people.

SATIN. Give it up! Why feel ashamed? – nobody's ashamed that your life's worse than a dog's, nobody gives a damn! Just think – if you stop working, and I stop, and hundreds of thousands of others stop – everyone, understand? – if everyone stops working, no one moves a finger . . . what'll happen then?

KLESHCH. They'll all die of hunger.

LUKA (*to* SATIN). You should join the Runners, the way you talk. (They're a sect that doesn't accept any earthly things. The police find them harmful – so they run.*)

SATIN. I know. They're no fools, grandpa.

From KOSTYLIOV's *window come* NATASHA's *screams.*

NATASHA (*off*). No! What for? What have I done!

LUKA (*anxiously*). Is that Natasha screaming? Oh God . . .

From the KOSTYLIOV *apartment, noise, sounds of struggle, broken crockery, and the high-pitched shouting of* KOSTYLIOV.

KOSTYLIOV. Oh – you – you heathen! you blasphemous whore! – you filthy slut!

VASSILISSA. Stop . . . wait . . . I'll get her . . . there . . . there . . .

NATASHA. Help! They're beating me, they'll kill me!

SATIN (*shouts in at the window*). Hey, you there . . . !

LUKA (*fussing*). Vasska . . . call Vasska . . . Oh God! Brothers . . . friends . . .

ACTOR (*running out*). I'll go . . . I'll get him . . .

BUBNOV. They beat her a lot these days.

SATIN. Come on, grandpa – we can be witnesses . . .

LUKA (*following* SATIN). What good would I be as a witness? No . . . better get Vasska as quick as possible . . . Tsk-tsk!

Exits tut-tutting behind SATIN.

NATASHA. No, Vassilissa! – aah – Vassi-aah . . .

BUBNOV. They've gagged her. I'm going to have a look.

The noise from the KOSTYLIOVS' *room dies down, apparently moving from the room into the hall. A shout from the old man of 'Stop!' A door slams loudly, cutting off the noise as if with an axe. On stage it is quiet. Evening twilight.* KLESHCH,

---

* This explanation of 'The Runners' is taken from Gorky's autobiographical volume *My Apprenticeships*.

taking no part, is sitting on the sledge. He rubs his hands hard,
starts muttering, unintelligibly at first, then:

KLESHCH. Well, what then? Got to live somehow. (*Loudly.*)
Got to have a place! Eh? – there's no place. Nothing. There's
nothing. A man's alone, that's what it comes to. Alone. No
help. There's no help.

He goes out slowly, head bowed.
A few seconds of sinister silence, then, somewhere in the passage,
vague noises start up, a chaos of sounds. It grows and comes
nearer. Individual voices can be heard.

VASSILISSA. I'm her sister! Let go of me!
KOSTYLIOV. What right have you got . . .?
VASSILISSA. Jailbird!
SATIN. Get Vasska – quickly – Zob – sock him!

A police whistle. The TARTAR runs out. His right hand is in a
sling. He is followed by KRIVOY ZOB and MEDVEDIEV.

TARTAR. What law say okay kill in daytime?
KRIVOY ZOB. Oh, I didn't half thump him!
MEDVEDIEV. You – how dare you – fighting like that!
TARTAR. And you, hey? What about your duty, hey?
MEDVEDIEV (*chasing* KRIVOY ZOB). Hey, stop! Give me back my
whistle!

KOSTYLIOV *runs on.*

KOSTYLIOV. Abram! Catch him! Take him! He's a killer . . .

From behind the corner appear KVASHNIA and NASTYA,
supporting NATASHA, bedraggled. SATIN comes on backwards,
pushing at VASSILISSA, who is waving her arms about,
attempting to get past him and hit her sister. ALYOSHKA is
jumping around her like one possessed, whistling in her ears,
shouting, howling. Subsequently a few more men and women
in rags crowd in through the corner.

SATIN (*to* VASSILISSA). Keep back, bloody screech-owl!

VASSILISSA. Get out of my way, jailbird! I'll tear that slut to ribbons if I have to die for it!

KVASHNIA *leads* NATASHA *out of range.*

KVASHNIA. Stop it now, Karpovna, you should be ashamed! Behaving like a wild beast!

MEDVEDIEV *catches hold of* SATIN.

MEDVEDIEV. Aha! Got you!

SATIN. Krivoy Zob – get at them! Vasska! Vasska!

They are all crowded together in swirling confusion in the entrance to the passageway. NATASHA *is led further away and set down on a pile of wood.* PEPEL *bursts through the crowd, out of the passageway, pushing everyone aside with powerful gestures, saying nothing.*

PEPEL. Where is she? Where's Natasha? You . . .

KOSTYLIOV *slips round the corner.*

KOSTYLIOV. Abram! Get Vasska! Help him, lads, help take Vasska, he's a robber, a thief.

PEPEL. Ah you . . . old bugger, you!

PEPEL *strikes* KOSTYLIOV *a powerful blow. The old man falls so that only the top half of him is visible round the corner.* PEPEL *rushes to* NATASHA.

VASSILISSA. Get him – get Vasska! Oh, my good friends, hit him, hit the thief!

MEDVEDIEV (*shouting at* SATIN). Keep out of this, this is a family affair, they're relations, what's it got to do with you?

PEPEL. How . . . what did she get you with? A knife?

KVASHNIA. [Just look at that,] look what the brutes did! Scalded the girl's legs with boiling water!

NASTYA. Tipped the samovar over her.

TARTAR. May be accident . . . got to know sure . . . not say if not know!

NATASHA (*almost fainting*). Vasska . . . take me away . . . hide me . . . I want to die!

VASSILISSA. Merciful heavens! Look – come and see – he's dead! He's been killed!

> *All crowd into the passageway around* KOSTYLIOV's *body.* BUBNOV *emerges from the crowd and crosses quickly to* PEPEL, *speaks to him in a low voice.*

BUBNOV. Vasska! The old rascal, he's – he's finished.

PEPEL (*staring at* BUBNOV *as if not understanding the words*). Go and call . . . we must get her to hospital. I'll deal with them.

BUBNOV. Listen, I tell you, someone's finished off the old man!

> *The noise on the stage dies down, like fire doused with water. Murmurs here and there, variously: 'He never is!' 'Oh Jesus' 'Hell!' 'Here, let's get out of here!' 'Bugger this!' 'Better watch out' 'Come on, let's get out before the police come!'* > *The crowd becomes smaller.* BUBNOV *and the* TARTAR *go out.* > NASTYA *and* KVASHNIA *rush over to* KOSTYLIOV's *body.*

VASSILISSA (*rising from the ground, shouting triumphantly*). They've killed him! They've killed my husband – and there – there's the one that did it! I saw him! Oh, my good friends, I did, I saw! Well, Vasska? It's the police now!

> PEPEL *moves away from* NATASHA.

PEPEL. Let go. Get away. (*He looks down at the body; to* VASSI-LISSA:) Well? Pleased? (*He touches the body with his foot.*) So the old dog dropped dead – it's worked out just the way you wanted. Huh! Why don't I do you in too?

> *He goes for her, and is grabbed quickly from behind by* SATIN *and* KRIVOY ZOB. VASSILISSA *hides in the passageway.*

SATIN. Have some sense, Vasska.

KRIVOY ZOB. Who-ah! Where are you galloping off to!

VASSILISSA (*reappearing*). Well, Vasska, my sweetheart? You won't escape what's coming to you! Police ...! Abram – blow your whistle!

MEDVEDIEV. They've snatched my whistle, the villains!

ALYOSHKA. Here it is.

> ALYOSHKA *blows the whistle;* MEDVEDIEV *gives chase.* SATIN *leads* PEPEL *back to* NATASHA.

SATIN. Nothing to be afraid of, Vasska – killing a man in a fight – it's nothing. They don't give you much for that.

VASSILISSA. Hold on to Vasska! He killed him! I saw!

SATIN. I hit the old fraud two or three times myself. He didn't need much to go down. Call me as a witness, Vasska.

PEPEL. I want – I don't want to clear myself – I just want to drag Vassilissa into it, and I will – I'll drag her in all right! This is just what she wanted – she tried to talk me into killing her husband, she'd been working on me to do it ...

NATASHA (*suddenly, loudly*). Ah – now I understand! So that's it, is it, Vasska? Listen, everyone – they were in it together, these two, my sister – and him! They're together! They arranged the whole thing! Isn't that right, Vasska? All you said to me earlier – it was just so she'd hear and ... Listen, everyone, she's his mistress, you all know that, and – and – they're in it together! She ... she talked him into it ... killing her husband ... he was in their way ... and I was in their way too so ... so they did this to me ...

PEPEL. Natasha! What are you – what ...?

SATIN. What the hell ...!

VASSILISSA. Liar! She's lying ... I ... he ... Vasska killed him!

NATASHA. They're in it together. God damn your souls, both of you!

SATIN. Jesus, what a performance! You watch out, Vasska, they'll drown you between the pair of them.

KRIVOY ZOB. Can't understand a word of it. Crazy business!

PEPEL. Natalia – you can't – mean all that? You can't believe I'm in with – her!

SATIN. For God's sake, Natasha – think!

VASSILISSA (*in the passage*). My husband's been killed, sir. It was Vasska Pepel, the thief, inspector, he killed him. I saw it, everyone saw it . . .

NATASHA (*throwing herself about, almost in a faint*). Listen, everyone . . . my sister and Vasska killed him! Listen, you policemen! [that one there, my sister, she coached him, she persuaded him . . . he's her lover . . . that's him, there, damn him!] They killed him . . . take them both . . . try them . . . take me too . . . take me to prison . . . Oh, for the love of Christ, take me to prison!

CURTAIN

Act Four

The same setting as the first Act, only Pepel's room is no longer there, the partition has been taken down. And in the place where Kleshch sat, the anvil has gone. In the corner where Pepel's room used to be the TARTAR *is lying, restlessly, groaning from time to time.* KLESHCH *is seated at the table, mending an accordion, now and again trying the notes. At the other end of the table,* SATIN, *the* BARON, *and* NASTYA. *In front of them, a bottle of vodka, three bottles of beer, a large hunk of black bread. On the stove the* ACTOR *is tossing restlessly and coughing. Night.*

The stage is lit by a lamp in the middle of the table. Noise of the wind outside.

KLESHCH. Yes . . . he took himself off while all that fuss was going on . . .

BARON. Melted before the police like . . . smoke before the fire.

SATIN. Even as sinners do flee before the face of the righteous.

NASTYA. He was a good old man! And you – you're not men, you're maggots.

BARON. Your health, mademoiselle!

SATIN. He was a funny old bugger all right. Nastionka even managed to fall in love with him.

NASTYA. Yes, I did fall in love with him. I do love him, it's quite true. He saw everything, understood everything . . .

SATIN (*laughing*). And altogether – for a lot of people – he was like pap for the toothless.

BARON (*laughing*). Like a poultice for boils!

KLESHCH. He – he had some pity. You lot haven't got an ounce of pity in you.

SATIN. What good will it do you if I pity you?

KLESHCH. At least you know how . . . well, I won't say pity, but you should know how not to hurt a person . . .

The TARTAR *sits up on his plank bed and rocks his wounded hand like a child.*

TARTAR. Old man was good. He has law in his soul. Who has law in his soul is good. Who loses law – loses his life.

BARON. What law, prince?

TARTAR. That one – different kinds – you know what.

BARON. Further, further!

TARTAR. Not to harm another being. That law.

SATIN. That's known as 'The Code of Criminal and Corrective Penalties.'

BARON. [Or sometimes – 'Statute of Penalties to be imposed by Provincial Magistrates'.]

TARTAR. Is called Koran . . . Your Koran must be law, soul must be Koran. Yes!

KLESHCH (*trying the accordion*). Still hissing, the bitch. But the prince is quite right. Man should live by the law. By the Gospel.

SATIN. Do it.

BARON. Try.

TARTAR. [Mahomet gave Koran and say, 'Here is law, do as written here.' One day time come when Koran not enough . . . that time must give own law, new law . . . Every time give its own law.

SATIN. Ab-so-lute-ly! A time came and gave us the 'Code of Penalties' – a nice tough law! You won't wear that one out in a hurry.]

NASTYA *suddenly bangs her glass down on the table.*

NASTYA. And why – why – do I go on living here? With you lot? What for? I'll go away . . . go off somewhere . . . to the ends of the earth!

BARON. With no shoes, mademoiselle?

NASTYA. Stark naked! I'll crawl on all fours!

BARON. How picturesque that will be, mademoiselle! On all fours . . .

NASTYA. I shall. I'll crawl. Anything not to have to see your ugly mug again . . . Oh, it all makes me so sick! All this . . . this whole life and . . . and everyone.

SATIN. If you do go, take the Actor along with you. He's thinking of going to the same place. He's heard that only half a mile or so from the ends of the earth there's a clinic for the treatment of organons . . .

The ACTOR *raises his head from the stove.*

ACTOR. Organisms – imbecile!

SATIN. For organons poisoned by alcohol. . . .

ACTOR. Yes! And he'll go there, too – he'll go, you wait and see.

BARON. And who is *he*, monsieur?

ACTOR. Me!

BARON. Grazie, good servant of the goddess – what's her name? The goddess of drama, tragedy? What was she called . . .?

ACTOR. The muse, idiot! Not a goddess – a muse!

SATIN. Lachesa, Here, Aphrodite, Atropos . . . God only knows . . . It's all the old man's doing, you know what I mean, Baron? He screwed the Actor up to this.

BARON. The old man's a fool.

ACTOR. Ignoramuses! Barbarians! Mel-po-me-na! Soulless wretches! He'll go – just you wait and see! 'Devour yourselves, benighted minds!' A poem by . . . Béranger. Yes! He'll find a place for himself where there's no . . . no . . .

BARON. Nothing at all, monsieur?

ACTOR. Yes! Nothing! 'This pit is all the grave I need, Here I die, a broken reed!' Why live at all? What for?

BARON. All right, Edmund Kean, [you dissipated genius –] that's enough of your yelling!

ACTOR. Rubbish! I shall yell!

NASTYA *raises her head from the table and makes a gesture of dismissal with both hands.*

NASTYA. Go on, shout away. You tell 'em.

BARON. Where's the sense of it, mademoiselle?

SATIN. Leave them, Baron. To hell with them! Let 'em shout, let 'em split their heads open, let 'em do it! There *is* sense to it ... don't interfere with a person, as the old man used to say ... It's him, old yeasty-beard, who's started all our lodgers fermenting.

KLESHCH. He set them off somewhere – but he never showed them the road.

BARON. The old man's a fake.

NASTYA. Liar! Fake yourself!

BARON. Down, mademoiselle!

KLESHCH. Didn't care for the truth, that old man ... dead set against the truth! Quite right too. What would we do with it if we had it? Even without it, we can't breathe! Look at the prince there – had his hand crushed at work, it's going to have to be cut right off, understand? Right off! There's the truth for you!

SATIN (*banging the table with his fist*). Shut up! You ... cattle! Sods! Shut up about the old man! (*More calmly.*) You, Baron – you're the worst of the lot. You don't understand anything about anything, you just talk rubbish! The old man is not a fake! [What ... is ... the truth? A human being – that's the truth! He understood that, and you don't. You're thick as bricks, the lot of you! I understand the old man ...] all right, yes, he lied – but that was out of pity for you, damn you! There are people, lots of people, who lie out of pity for their neighbour. I know about that – I've read books – and their lies are beautiful, inspired, exciting! They have a lie that comforts, that – that reconciles ... But there's another lie. It's – it can justify the load that crushed a workman's hand, and it – it blames the man who's dying of hunger! I know that lie! Whoever's weak in the soul, and lives off the sap of others, he needs that lie. Some are supported by the lie, others hide themselves away underneath it ... but whoever's his own master, independent, not leeching on someone else – what does he need a lie for? Lies – they're the religion of slaves and bosses! The only god for a free man is the truth.

BARON. Bravo! Well said! I agree! Spoken like a gentleman!

SATIN. Why shouldn't a cheat speak like a gentleman when gentlemen speak like cheats? Yes, I've forgotten a lot, but I still know something. The old man? He's a clever one. He scoured my soul the way acid scours a dirty old coin – let's drink to his health! Fill 'em up!

NASTYA *pours some beer and gives it to* SATIN.

(*Smiling.*) The old man lives from what's in himself – looks at everything with his own eyes. Once I asked him – Grandpa, what do people live for?

He tries to imitate LUKA's *voice and mannerisms.*

'Ah', he says, 'Ah, now, people live for something better, brotherkin. Now you take some carpenters, let's say, a lot of carpenters and all their rubbishy stuff. And now, from among this lot, there's born a carpenter – ah, such a carpenter as never before was seen on this earth, there's not another carpenter to match him! He makes his mark on the entire carpentry trade – and straightway it moves forward twenty years! Better, every last one of them! It's the same with all the others, locksmiths, if you like, cobblers, bakers, the rest of the workers . . . and all the peasants . . . and even the gentry . . . all living for something better! Each one of them thinks he's living just for himself, and it turns out he's living for something better! Each one of them living on for a hundred years or more – for the sake of a better man!

NASTYA *gazes into* SATIN's *face.* KLESHCH *stops working on the accordion and also listens. The* BARON, *head bowed low, drums with his fingers quietly on the table. The* ACTOR, *emerging from the stove, is about to climb carefully on to the plank bed.*

'Everyone, brotherkin, everyone there is, lives towards something better! That's why every soul must be respected, for it's not for us to know who he is, what he was born for or what he may do ... maybe he was born for our happiness, to bring some sort of good to us? Above all, the children must be respected – the little ones! The little ones need *space*! Don't interfere with them, don't hinder them in their living ... respect the childerkin!'

SATIN *laughs. A pause.*

BARON (*thoughtfully*). Mm – yes ... for something better, eh? Reminds me of my own family ... an old name – dates from the time of Catherine the Great – nobles, warriors ... an old French line. They served the Czar, rose higher and higher ... Under Nicholas the First my grandfather, Gustave Debile, held – uh – a post – most important post ... yes – wealth ... hundreds of serfs ... horses ... chefs ...

NASTYA. Liar! There was not!

BARON (*jumping up*). Wha-a-at! Well ... further!

NASTYA. None of it happened!

BARON (*shouting*). A house in Moscow! A house in Petersburg! Carriages – carriages with coats of arms!

KLESHCH *picks up the accordion, walks over to one side, watches the scene from there.*

NASTYA. Never happened.

BARON. Down! I tell you – dozens of lackeys!

NASTYA (*with relish*). Not true.

BARON. I'll kill you!

NASTYA (*making as if to run away*). There weren't any carriages!

SATIN. Stop it, Nastionka! don't tease him.

BARON. Wait – listen – you little bitch! – my grandfather ...

NASTYA. No grandfather – no carriage – no lackeys – nothing!

SATIN *roars with laughter. The* BARON, *tired from his burst of temper, sits down on a bench.*

BARON. Satin ... tell her ... tell that whore ... Are you laughing too? Don't you believe me either?

He shouts with despair, banging his fists on the table.

There *was*, damn and blast the lot of you!

NASTYA (*triumphantly*). A-ha, you can howl, too! Now you know what it's like when you're not believed!

KLESHCH (*returning to the table*). I thought there was going to be a fight.

TARTAR. O-oh, stupid people! Very bad!

BARON. I – I cannot permit anyone to mock me! I have ... proof ... documents, damn it!

SATIN. Throw them away! And forget about grandpapa's carriages – they won't take you anywhere now.

BARON. But still, how *dare* she ...

NASTYA. Just listen – how dare I!

SATIN. You see – she dares. Why not? Is she any worse than you? She may not have any carriages or grandfathers – probably not even a father or a mother – but ...

BARON (*calming down*). Damn you, Satin – you know how to discuss things calmly ... I don't seem to have any character.

SATIN. Acquire some. It comes in handy.

Pause.

Nastya – are you going to the hospital?

NASTYA. What for?

SATIN. To see Natasha.

NASTYA. Come on! She's been out of there for ages – came out, and just disappeared. Vanished.

SATIN. So she's gone for good.

KLESHCH. Wonder whose axe will go deepest – Vasska's into Vassilissa, or hers into him?

NASTYA. Vassilissa's bound to snake out of it somehow – she's crafty. And Vasska will get sent to forced labour.

SATIN. It's only prison if you kill in the course of a fight.

NASTYA. Pity. Forced labour's what he needs – you all ought to be sent to forced labour ... sweep you up like a pile of rubbish and into the rubbish pit with you!

SATIN (*surprised*). What's got into you? Gone out of your mind?

BARON. Oh, now I'm going to box her ears for her damned impudence!

NASTYA. You try! Just you touch me!

BARON. I will, I'll ...

SATIN. Pack it in! Keep your hands off her ... don't interfere with a person! I just can't get that old man out my head! (*Laughs.*) Don't interfere with a person – and if I've been interfered with once and for all ... what do I do? Forgive? Never. Nobody. Not for a thing.

BARON (*to* NASTYA). You've got to understand that you're not my equal. You're just ... dirt.

NASTYA. You poor idiot, aren't you living off of me like a maggot off an apple?

A friendly burst of laughter from the men.

KLESHCH. Oh you fool! Some apple!

BARON. One really can't be angry – she's such an idiot!

NASTYA. Laughing, are you? Liar! – you don't really think it's funny!

ACTOR (*gloomily*). Go on – bowl them down.

NASTYA. If only I could I'd –

She takes a cup from the table and smashes it to the ground.

– that's what I'd do to you!

TARTAR. Why breaks pots? Eh – stupid!

BARON (*getting up*). No, now I really must teach her some manners.

NASTYA (*running off*). You go to hell!

SATIN (*calling after her*). Hey, that'll do! Who are you trying to scare? What's all this about?

NASTYA. Dogs! May you all drop dead, dogs!

ACTOR (*gloomily*). Amen!

TARTAR. O-oh, Russian woman – savage woman! Rude ... free! Tartar woman not – Tartar woman know Tartar law!

KLESHCH. She needs a good hiding.

BARON (*hisses*). S-s-s-slut!

> KLESHCH *tries out the accordion.*

KLESHCH. Finished! No sign of the owner, though. The little fellow's out on the tiles again.

SATIN. Now – have a drink!

KLESHCH. Thanks. Time to turn in, then.

SATIN. Getting used to us?

> KLESHCH *drains his cup, then goes over to his plank bed in the corner.*

KLESHCH. It's all right. There's people all over the place. You don't see it at first, but then ... you take a closer look ... turns out they're all human ... all of them all right, really ...

> *The* TARTAR *spreads something out on his plank bed, kneels down, prays. The* BARON *points to the* TARTAR, *addressing* SATIN.

BARON. Look.

SATIN. Leave him. He's all right, don't interfere with him. (*Laughs.*) I'm in a kind mood today, God knows why!

BARON. You're always kind when you've been drinking. Kind – and clever.

SATIN. When I'm drunk – I like everything! Mmm-ye-e-es. So – he's praying? Fine – a man can believe, or not believe – that's up to him. Man is free. Whatever he does, he has to pay for himself – for believing, for not believing, for loving, for thinking – man pays for it all himself, and that's why he's free. Man! There's the truth for you! What is Man? It isn't me – or you – or them ... no! It's you and me and them and the old man and Mahomet ... all rolled into one! (*He draws the figure of a man in the air.*) You see? It's tremendous! All the beginnings and all the ends are here – everything, in Man – everything, for Man! Only Man exists, everything else is the work of his hand and brain! Hu-man-kind! – it's magnificent! It sounds so proud! Man! Man ... must be respected – not pitied, not humiliated with pity! Respected! Let's drink to Man, Baron! (*He stands up*.) Ah, but it's good – to feel you're a man! I'm an old lag, a murderer, a cardsharper – well, yes, all right. When I walk along the street, people [see me as a crook, and edge away. They] glance back over their shoulders at me . . . and sometimes they shout, 'Layabout! Bum! Get some work!' Work? What for? To stuff my gut full of food? (*He laughs*.) I've always despised people who worry too much about being well-fed – that's not the point, Baron! That's not the point! Man is above that . . . man is above . . . being well-fed!

BARON (*shaking his head*). You can work things out – that's good. It must warm the heart. I don't have that . . . I . . . can't. (*He looks round – in a low, careful voice*.) I feel scared, dear chap . . . sometimes. D'you understand? I'm afraid! Because . . . what . . . further . . . is there?

SATIN (*walking about*). Rubbish! Who is there to be afraid of?

BARON. You know, ever since I can remember . . . there's always been a sort of fog in my head. I've never understood anything. I feel . . . out of place . . . somehow. I seem to have done nothing all my life but change one lot of clothes for another. And what for? – I don't understand it! I went to school, wore the uniform of the Noblemen's Academy . . . but what did I study? Don't remember. Got married – put on a frock coat, then a dressing-gown . . . married some nasty female – what was that about? I don't understand. I went through my fortune, ended up wearing some sort of old grey coat and faded trousers . . . and how did I come to be ruined? Never noticed. I worked in the department of the exchequer, wore a uniform with a cockade on my cap . . . helped myself to a bit of public money . . . then they dressed me in convict's overalls . . . finally put on these things. And it's all passed like a dream . . . Well? Does that seem – ridiculous?

SATIN. Not really. Stupid, more like.

BARON. Yes. I think it's stupid, too. But I must have been born for some reason, mustn't I?

SATIN (*laughing*). Very likely. Man is born – for something better!
(*He nods.*) Yes, that's – that's good.

BARON. That Nastya – where did she run off to? I'd better go and
see. After all, she . . .

The BARON *exits. Pause.*

ACTOR. Tartar!

Pause.

Prince!

The TARTAR *turns his head.*

Pray for me.

TARTAR. What?

ACTOR (*quietly*). Pray . . . for me.

TARTAR (*after a moment's silence*). Pray for yourself.

The ACTOR *climbs quickly down from the stove, goes over to the
table, pours some vodka with a trembling hand, drinks it – and
almost runs into the hall.*

ACTOR. Going . . . gone!

SATIN. Hey – you – sycambro! Where?

SATIN whistles. Enter MEDVEDIEV, *in a woman's padded
jerkin, and* BUBNOV, *carrying a bundle of pretzel rolls in one
hand and some fish in the other; a bottle of vodka is under his
arm, another in his jacket pocket.*

MEDVEDIEV. The camel, now – the camel is a sort of donkey.
Only without ears.

BUBNOV. Shut up. You're a sort of donkey yourself.

MEDVEDIEV. The camel – has no ears at all. He hears with his
nostrils.

BUBNOV (*to* SATIN). My friend! – I've been looking for you under
every barrel in town! [Take a bottle, my hands are full.

SATIN. If you put the rolls down on the table you'd have one
hand free.

BUBNOV. True.] Hey – you – Sheriff! Look – there he is, our own clever boy!

MEDVEDIEV. Crooks are all clever – don't I know it! [They have to be. A good man's still good even if he's stupid, but a bad one – has simply got to be clever.] But about the camel . . . you're wrong, you know. He's a riding animal. Hasn't got any horns . . . nor any teeth . . .

BUBNOV. Where is everyone? Why's nobody here? Hey, come on out, it's my treat! Who's that in the corner?

SATIN. How soon will you have drunk yourself into the gutter? Scarecrow!

BUBNOV. Soon enough. This time I've amassed a . . . modest little capital. Krivoy Zob! Where's Krivoy Zob?

KLESHCH *comes up the table.*

KLESHCH. Not here.

BUBNOV. Grrr-uff! Grrr-uff! Down, you old watchdog! Don't bark, don't growl – sing, enjoy yourself, keep that old snout out of the dirt! Come on, it's my treat – I like to treat . . . *everyone*! If I was rich I'd . . . keep a free bar! Yes, before God I would! – with music and – and – fine singers! Come on, I'd say, drink up, all of you, eat, [let's have some songs,] let yourselves go! Roll up, you poor devils, roll up to my free bar! [Satin! I'd . . . for you I'd . . . Here, look – take half of my entire capital . . . there . . . just like that!

SATIN. Give me the lot, straight off.

BUBNOV. All my capital? Straight off? All right – here! – one rouble . . . and another . . . twenty kopecks . . . a five . . . a two . . . that's the lot.]

SATIN. [Fine. It'll be safer with me. I'll put it on a card.

MEDVEDIEV. I'm a witness to that. Money's been handed over for safe-keeping, to the tune of . . . how much was it?

BUBNOV. You're a camel, not a witness. We don't need witnesses.]

ALYOSHKA *enters, barefoot.*

ALYOSHKA. Comrades! . . . I've got my feet wet!

BUBNOV. Come on and get your throat wet. That'll fix you. You're a nice lad – you play and sing, and that's good. But you drink too much. It's bad for you, brother – drinking's bad for you!

ALYOSHKA. I can see that from you. You're only human when you're drunk. Kleshch! Have you mended my squeeze-box?

He sings, dancing a few steps.

> Oh, if this old mug
> Weren't so fine to see
> My sister wouldn't open
> Her legs for me!

I'm frozen, brothers. It's c-c-c-cold!

MEDVEDIEV. H'm. And might I ask – who is your sister?

BUBNOV. Leave him be. You've had your lot, brother, you're not Sheriff any longer. It's all finished. Not a policeman, and not an uncle.

ALYOSHKA. But just – auntie's husband!

BUBNOV. One of your nieces is in jail. The other's dying.

MEDVEDIEV (*disdainfully*). Nonsense! She is not dying. She has . . . disappeared without trace.

SATIN *laughs.*

BUBNOV. It's all the same, brother! No nieces, no uncle!

ALYOSHKA. Your Excellency! Retired drummer-boy to the regimental goat – sah!

> Oh I'm merry and good
> But I haven't a bean
> My sister's got the lolly
> And she's my queen!

It's cold.

Enter KRIVOY ZOB; *then, and until the end of the Act, a few more men and women. They take their coats off, lie down on the plank beds, and grumble.*

KRIVOY ZOB. Bubnov! Why did you run away?

BUBNOV. Come here! Sit down ... let's have a song, brother! Our favourite, all right?

TARTAR. Is night. Must sleep! Sing songs in day.

SATIN. Ah, never mind that, prince! You come over here.

TARTAR. How, never mind? Is noisy. When people sing, is always noisy.

BUBNOV (*going over to him*). How's the hand, prince? Have they cut it off?

TARTAR. What for, cut off? Better wait. Maybe not have to cut off. A hand not iron, to be cut off so easy.

KRIVOY ZOB. You're finished, Assanka. Without a hand you're nothing, useless. Us sort, we're only wanted for our hands and our backs – no hand, no man! Your life's a clinker. Come and have some vodka – there's nothing else.

KVASHNIA *enters.*

KVASHNIA. Ah, my dear little lodgers! Ooh, but outside there, outside! It's so cold and slushy ... Is my little Sheriff here? Constable!

MEDVEDIEV. Here.

KVASHNIA. You traipsing about in my jacket again? You look as if you're a bit ... Well? What do you think you're up to?

MEDVEDIEV. It's on account of ... it's Bubnov's nameday ... and ... er ... it's cold, sleety ...

KVASHNIA. You watch it now – sleety indeed! None of your tricks, just you get off to bed.

MEDVEDIEV (*going into the kitchen*). Bed – I can do that all right. I want to. It's time.

SATIN. Do you have to be so strict with him?

KVASHNIA. No good being any other way, my friend. A husband like that – he has to be dealt with firmly. I took him on as a partner, thought he'd be useful, him being a policeman, with you rowdy lot to handle, and me only a woman ... And what does he do? Drinks! That's no good to me!

SATIN. You chose yourself a bad partner.

KVASHNIA. There wasn't a better one going ... You wouldn't want to live with me – indeed you wouldn't! And if you did, inside a week you'd have lost me at cards – me and all my trash.

SATIN (*laughing*). It's true enough, landlady! I'd lose you ...

KVASHNIA. There you are. Alyoshka!

ALYOSHKA. Here [he is! Me!]

KVASHNIA. What's this you've [been tittle-tattling about me?

ALYOSHKA. Me? Everything! Most conscientiously, everything – just as I see it! Now there, I say – there's a woman! Wonderful! Meat, fat and bones, all twenty-five stone of it, and not one ounce of brain among it!

KVASHNIA. Ah, now, there you're quite wrong! I've got plenty of brain! Well – and why've you] been saying that I beat my little policeman?

ALYOSHKA. I thought you were beating him that time you pulled him down by his hair.

KVASHNIA (*laughing*). Idiot! As if you didn't see! Anyway, why wash dirty linen in public? It hurts his pride – it's because of your silly tales he's started drinking.

ALYOSHKA. So it's true what they say – even camels drink!

SATIN *and* KLESHCH *laugh.*

KVASHNIA. Always poking fun, aren't you? What sort of a man are you, Alyoshka?

ALYOSHKA. Absolutely top quality type man! Of all trades, Ma'am. Wherever I look, there I'm took!

BUBNOV (*beside* TARTAR's *plank bed*). Come on, join us. We're not going to let anyone sleep, anyway. We're going to sing ... all night long! Zob!

KRIVOY ZOB. Sing? Ay, it's possible.

ALYOSHKA. And I – will accompany you!

SATIN. And we'll listen!

TARTAR (*smiling*). Well, shaitan Bubna, bring out your vodka! We drink, we make merry, and if death come – we bury!

BUBNOV. Pour him a drink, Satin! Zob, sit down! Well, brothers – a man doesn't need much, does he? Here I am, I've had a drink – and I'm happy! Zob – begin! Our favourite! When I start singing . . . I shall cry.

KRIVOY ZOB (*sings*). 'Though the bright sun may be shining . . .'

BUBNOV (*joining in*). 'My dungeon stays as dark as night . . .'

The door is suddenly opened. The BARON *stands in the doorway and shouts.*

BARON. Hey . . . you . . . come . . . come here! Out there . . . in the yard . . . the Actor . . . He's hanged himself!

Silence. All look at the BARON. *From behind his back* NASTYA *appears, and, slowly, her eyes wide open, makes her way to the table.*

SATIN (*quietly*). Ooh . . . spoilt our song . . . the *fool*!

CURTAIN

Music and full text of the song sung by BUBNOV and KRIVOY ZOB in Acts Two and Four.

Though the bright sun may be shining
My dungeon stays as dark as night
The prison guard stands by my window – oh – oh –
And with his body steals my light.

Guard me, though I need no guarding,
I can't hope to break this chain,
But stand aside from my small window – oh – oh –
That I may see the sun again.

Oh you chain, you heavy mooring,
Oh you cru-el iron bond,
I can never shake nor break you – oo – oo –
And roam the sunlit world beyond.